I0694568

BRIDES IN THE DARK

A NEW FAIRY TALE

JACOB STEVEN MOHR

Brides in the Dark: a new fairy tale
written by Jacob Steven Mohr
published by Quill & Crow Publishing House

Cover Art by Jorge Mascarenhas / Formatting by Fay Lane

Edited by Lisa Morris, Mathew L Reyes

Printed in the United States of America

ISBN: 978-1-967911-12-7

ISBN: 978-1-967911-11-0 (ebook)

Publisher's Website: www.quillandcrowpublishinghouse.com

For my mother, the toughest and fiercest she-bat of them all.

My sister, my friend...

Today I'm sending a gift to you. I have no tongue to name him, and no wings to deliver him into your arms. But he is my son, born out of my own selfish need—for something to love, something that was not myself.

Today he's no longer my child, but a Man—but I have loved him, I think, into something more. In form and temper, he is so much like them, but in his heart, he belongs with us.

He can be a tool in our hands. He can be our rescue.

If you allow it—by your side, he could even become more.

There's a chance, sister, we may again soar side by side. But it will have to be carefully done. You'll need to be gentle with him, as he's never flown these skies before in his life. I've taught him as much as I could and loved him as much as I could, but it won't be enough. I was not enough.

For good or for ill, you two must navigate this darkness alone.

CHAPTER 1

THE SAME WOLF

HE SAW the wolf from a long way off. The north pasture was wide and sloping, with no trees to break up its loneliness. There was nowhere a predator could conceal itself but inside the gathering darkness. For now, the evening sun still burned the horizon, and the wolf made no effort to hide itself. It circled the herd, its pace languid and its snout uptilted, scenting the cool late air. The flock fled uphill in a rolling white wave.

Patrick set aside his crook and drew his spyglass.

It was the same wolf; he was sure of it.

He'd discovered the first carcass two dawns before. An old, sickly ewe—her throat torn out and her black tongue lolling, wool matted brown and pink. The second misty morning had yielded a lamb, or what was left of a lamb. She was only scraps when Patrick found her, scattered near a ridge of toothy rocks at the pasture's edge. Only the head was left intact, with one black and bulging eye rolled up toward the climbing sun. All around this, huge pawprints pockmarked the mud.

The wolf had taken two sheep in two nights. There could not be a third.

Patrick held his breath. The lens of the spyglass swept across the vast green landscape. The wind was in his ears, and the groaning of the sheep. They bunched together, their black faces pointing out in a ring. In the dark, they would be defenseless—and Patrick, blind in that same dark, would be helpless as well. His hands trembled in anticipation as he watched the wolf lope closer, winding up the slope, its wicked, smiling jaw open and panting. Against the grass, its body was a shadow rippling over the land. It slunk nearer and nearer to the outcrop of stones where Patrick had encountered the lamb's body.

It vanished behind them—one second passed, then two. There was a hard snap of metal, a high, quick scream of pain. Black-tufted limbs thrashed. Then, stillness everywhere.

Patrick leapt up from his crouch, gathering Old Matthew's cloak around him. Running down the gentle slope was like flying or falling—the wind flapped the heavy wool behind him like one great wing. He'd abandoned the spyglass beside his wicker basket but kept his shepherd's crook in his fist. As he approached the rocks, he slowed, listening. Just beyond the outcrop, he heard throaty growls and heavy panting breaths, just under the wind's distant moan.

He crept closer, tender-footed, circling on tiptoe.

The wolf lay struggling in the trap. Iron jaws clamped shut on two of its legs, one in front and one in back, pinching the beast into a crooked letter C. Sharp metal teeth bit into the beast's flesh, sinking down to the bone. Hot dark blood steamed on the dirt and rocks. Despite these wounds, it was still a magnificent sight. Fur the color of bonfire smoke stretched over smooth, muscular flanks—eyes full of cold, intelligent hate, and fear, and desperate hunger. As Patrick edged nearer, it tried to leap up, foaming and snapping. But the trap's weight jerked it back, and it fell to earth once more, sprawled on one side, quick panicked breaths churning the air.

"What am I going to do with you?" Patrick murmured.

The wolf's black lips pulled back over yellow teeth; its tail lashed the mud.

He regarded the animal carefully, leaning on his

crook. It was smaller than he'd estimated when he laid the trap, a yearling pup, perhaps a season older or younger—though its fangs were no duller for it, or its bite gentler. But now an unpleasant chore lay ahead, and sickness twisted in the pit of Patrick's belly over it. He went to the outcrop, wrenching loose one large mossy stone, nearly as big around as his own head. He tested its weight in his hands. There was still light on the horizon, dripping down from the high rocky ridges surrounding Blackfrye. But the air was growing dark now, and colder with every passing moment.

The wolf looked up at him from the mud through one eye, its flank heaving.

It was a magnificent animal. But it had taken two sheep.

Patrick lifted the stone high over his head, then brought it down hard.

By the time he'd finished covering the corpse, night had swept down into the valley. It wasn't a proper grave —only a few loose stones to hide the wolf's carcass from scavengers that might damage the valuable pelt. But when he was finished, he stood over the mound, tracing a hasty blessing in the air with two scabby fingers. That's when he heard Rowan's low *halloo* and saw his yellow lantern bouncing up the slope toward him through the twilight.

"The whole village is gathered at your father's house," his cousin told him, panting from the trek up the rise. "They're all asking for you—drunk as lords, every one of them."

Rowan's face was a nest of dancing shadows. With his lantern clutched under his chin, his eyes were little more than ragged pools collected in his skull, and his massive shoulders looked like just another distant mountain guarding the valley. He angled his gaze downward, casting his lantern's orange glow on the stones piled at their feet.

"No trouble here?" he asked.

Patrick tucked his trembling hands fast to his sides. It had taken more than one blow with the rock to kill the creature. After the first, it had leapt up snarling— its jaws had missed Patrick's fingers by a whisper, closing instead on his shirtsleeve. Now it hung in tatters around his slender wrist, and he could still feel hot breath against his skin.

"No trouble," Patrick answered, shaking his head. "I left my lantern up the slope with my other things—I'll go fetch it, then meet the others."

"No need." Rowan thrust his own lantern forward. "Take mine. I'll stay with the flock tonight and all tomorrow as well. Old Matthew's arranged everything. You'll need proper rest tonight," —his expression changed in the dark— "with such a long climb ahead of you."

Patrick's pulse quickened, the wolf momentarily forgotten.

"Tomorrow, then?" he asked. "You're certain?"

"Am I certain, he asks." Rowan grinned, then suddenly crushed Patrick in a deep embrace. "I told you, it's all arranged. My little cousin's going to be a married man."

Patrick returned the hug, then squirmed free and scooped the lantern up. Saying his hurried thanks to Rowan, he started down the grassy slope, picking his way past jutting stones and patches of loose mud. Below him danced Blackfrye's merry lights—and already, the sound of music and men's voices in a mighty chorus.

"A word of advice, cousin!" Rowan called after him.

Patrick paused. "What's that now?"

He could hear the smirk in the older man's voice. "From a man who knows. Wash your hands before you go to meet your bride. They say they can smell blood from miles away. It drives them to frenzy—and what a honeymoon that might make you both!"

Patrick blushed. He resumed his hike down toward the lights, Rowan's bellowing laughter following him every step. It did nothing to dampen his anticipation or cool the flash of his blood. Nothing could, nothing in the whole world.

Nothing—except the memory of hot angry breath against his knuckles, and the crunch of bone, and the crackle and stretch of dried blood between every finger.

CHAPTER 2

THE COMPANY OF MEN

HE WASHED his hands in a cool basin by the back door of Old Matthew's house. The blood came off his fingers in flakes, sticking under his nails. Inside, deep voices rose in a tremendous chorus. Somebody had a fiddle playing, and the rest of the men sang along in slipshod harmonies and stomped the floorboards. Old Matthew's voice boomed above them all, half-singing, half-shouting instructions to the others.

"Louder!" he thundered. "Come on, I know you can sing louder than that. Look at you all—drinking my wine and eating my wife's food. This is how you welcome my son?"

Patrick pushed through the door, ducking his head when a few eyes in the warm greatroom turned his direction. It looked like every living soul in the village was there, packed in tight like apples in a barrel. Thick-armed Blackfrye men and their sons—and their son's sons, in more than a few instances. Their wives clung close, lips pressed together in mute red lines, following Patrick with their ink-well eyes. With their identical pale faces and lustrous black locks and slender frames, it was like being observed by a shelf of dolls. Only one stood unaccompanied—a taller beauty, whose rippling hair covered one cast-downward eye. She belonged to Rowan, still afield with the flock.

Patrick said a few *hellos*, shook a few hands, and ruffled the hair of a few younger boys who ran up to him, grinning with questions or a bite of food. Then he shouldered through the crowd to the great stone fire-place, where Old Matthew held court.

His father was not so old as his name suggested. Old Matthew's own father still drew breath—on his second bride at that, and still firm as oak timbers. But his rusted beard and wind-scraped face gave him the look of a seasoned general, or at least a gristly fisherman. It didn't hurt that calling him *Old Matthew* distinguished him from Young Matthew, another of Patrick's many cousins in the village. All Blackfrye men were cousins in some fashion, considering that their wives were all like enough to sisters.

And whatever military bearing his father might have achieved naturally was only increased by his bad eye. A lambskin patch covered its ruin, and Patrick had never been allowed to glimpse what lay beneath, though long puckering scars could be seen reaching out above and below. The other eye was a sharp and severe blue. As a boy, Patrick had believed he could feel that eye's stare burning him no matter where he was in the house, though this feeling had lessened somewhat as he grew older.

Now he approached his father, who rose up from his enormous armchair with hands spread wide. They clasped arms, and Old Matthew's lips brushed the top of his head.

"It's dead, then?" he murmured, so only they two could hear.

Patrick nodded. His hands, now clean, no longer shook.

Old Matthew pulled back and smiled.

"That's well handled. A man does what he must—and you *are* a man today."

Then he stepped forward, tipped his head back, and bellowed over the crowd. "My son," he repeated, "is a man today!"

The Blackfrye men's voices died away. Whoever had the fiddle laid it aside, and excepting the sounds of a few smaller boys nudging each other, Old Matthew's greatroom took on the somber atmosphere of a church. It was then that Patrick noticed movement from the back of the room. His mother had emerged from the kitchen, carrying a wooden platter piled with more food. Two white ribbons pulled back her dark hair, and she wore a white apron with flowers embroidered all across the stomach. She turned toward him. Their eyes met, and he waited for her to smile. Instead, she only stared. One hand lifted off the platter and lay over her bosom, then a finger pressed against her red lips.

The gesture left him puzzled. For just as long as he'd lived, Patrick had never heard his mother's voice. No wife in Blackfrye had ever spoken a word.

His mother slipped in among the crowd. Patrick's senses returned, and he realized nearly too late that his father had been addressing the throng. He perked up his head, trying to appear as though he'd been listening the whole time.

"...a joyful marriage," Old Matthew was saying —*preaching*, rather, as he so enjoyed when he had an audience of captives and a few drinks tucked away in his taut, round belly. "It means a joyful family. And the family is the strong stone brick by which we build our lives in this valley. Am I wrong?"

The room called back in one voice: "NO."

"Are we Wicke men," Old Matthew asked, "who hunt their wives in the forests?"

The house repeated its rebuttal.

"Are we Burning Coast fishmongers, who haul them up from the sea?"

Again, the gathered menfolk denied it. Old Matthew smiled. He threw a heavy arm across his son's shoulders, pulling him close and pressing the other hand to his boy's chest.

"We Blackfrye men, we choose our brides carefully," he boomed. "So our families stay strong, so our village keeps growing. Tomorrow, before dawn, my son will forge another link in that iron chain. Scale the mountain, call down a bride of his own, bring her here, to live among us. With a wife by his side, he'll join the ranks of men at last."

Old Matthew leaned close, so close Patrick smelled the wine on his breath.

"Now, tell us," his father said. "What gift will you bring your future bride?"

All those eyes on him made Patrick sweat. When he gave his father his answer, he whispered without meaning to. Old Matthew grimaced and rolled his eyes.

"You're a man today, for heaven's sake. Talk like it."

Nodding apologetically, Patrick cleared his throat. "A...a pot of honey."

"A pot of honey!" Old Matthew repeated, as though the other men hadn't heard. "And tell us this as well. Why have you chosen this offering for yourself?"

Patrick hesitated again. For months, he'd nibbled at the edges of this piece of the puzzle—what sort of wife *should* he want? But nobody he'd spoken to had seemed able or willing to answer him straight on. So instead, he simply shrugged.

"I...I want a sweet wife."

"A sweet wife!" Old Matthew bellowed. "Do you hear this?" He guffawed, leaning forward and smacking his palm against his thigh, and the other men laughed with him. A few pulled their brides close, nuzzling bearded faces against their cheeks or into the hollows of paper-colored necks. Their laughter had a coarse texture, like running one's hand over sawdust.

"Now, men of Blackfrye," Patrick's father continued his address to the crowd. "Answer me this. Has my son chosen rightly?"

"HE HAS," the house thundered.

"Is my son a man today?" roared Old Matthew.

The answer was not words, but a witless roar that swelled up from every corner of the room. Hands clapped; heavy boots stomped the floorboards. The house's very timbers shook with the strength and fury of men. Patrick looked across the sea of faces, feeling like they all had surged forward and swept him up onto their shoulders. Heat blossomed in the middle of his chest, and he finally let himself smile.

"Somebody get him a drink!" his father commanded.

Instantly, a half-dozen fists thrust a half-dozen cups of wine under Patrick's nose. He took the fullest of the offerings and thanked the man offering it. Old Matthew put heavy hands on his shoulders and forced him forward into the crowd, where more than a few other hands slapped his back, nearly making him spill his drink down his own shirtfront.

Patrick didn't mind it. Today, he was a man. And the more of his father's cold wine he drank, the more of a man he felt like. But as he found himself shunted between group after small group of grinning, flushed faces, his gaze kept straying to the corners of the room, for any empty space not filled by a bearded Blackfrye man. The wives all stared back at him with those same dark searching eyes, those same expressionless mouths.

But his mother wasn't among them. She was nowhere.

CHAPTER 3

HONEY AND DEAD FLOWERS

THE HOUSE BULGED with guests until well after midnight. And when all the songs were sung and all the congratulations given, and Patrick at last staggered down the hall to his own small bed, more swallows of wine had passed between his lips than he cared to count.

In the dark, his room swam. Shadows whirled and leapt, but he didn't bother lighting the lamp beside his bed. He simply crawled under the sheets, feeling beneath him for the rucksack he'd prepared before he left for the pasture that morning. Inside was the pot of honey and its dipping ladle, as well as a few other provisions for the long journey to come.

His eyes shut nearly the instant his head touched the pillow. But when he woke, there was no light in his window, and his bedside lamp sputtered. His mother had appeared in his room, sitting in his chair, with its back pressed against the shut door.

Patrick sat up and rubbed his eyes. In the flickering light, shadow-fingers tickled along the walls. In her long white linen nightgown, with her dark haunted eyes, his mother was every inch a ghastly apparition, an avenging specter. For the second time that day, she pressed a silencing finger to her lips. Something dangled limp from her other hand.

"What is it, Mother?" he whispered in a dry throat.

Of course, Patrick's mother didn't speak to answer him. But Old Matthew was an important man in Black-frye and had many duties that kept him away from the house, so Patrick had spent much of his boyhood by her side, even once he was weaned from her breast. He learned long ago to understand his mother in other ways, from expressions and signs and subtle gestures. So when she removed her finger from her lips and indicated the rucksack under his bed, Patrick obeyed her as though she'd spoken the command aloud. He pulled it into his lap and opened it, spreading the contents on the blanket beside him.

Patrick's mother stole forward on silent feet, scooping up the honey pot. She gave the sealed lid a suspicious sniff before she thrust it forward at her son, shaking her head so her long black hair swept across her shoulders like branches brushing against a window in the night.

"You don't like it?" he asked. Again, she shook her head.

It'll bring you a wife, her eyes instructed him. *But not the wife you want.*

Patrick examined the honey, its fine dark luster, the inviting gleam of the glass.

"Well—what do you know about it?" he grouched. Somebody was mining in his skull with picks and hammers, and he wanted to lay his head down again, to disrupt their industry.

She only shook her head again, then put the pot aside. She then pushed something else forward, the mysterious item she'd brought with her on her after-dark sojourn, rustling it under his nose. He took it from her gingerly. At first, it was only a bundle of grasses tied together loosely with thin string. But when he held them nearer to the sputtering lamp, he saw among the longer blades a few straight stems of a flowering plant he could not name, with heavy buds nodding shut-tight eyes atop them.

He glanced at his mother. She stared into him, nodding intently.

These, her tapping hand said. *These will call your bride to you.*

Patrick scratched the back of his neck. "Mother, I don't know..."

These, she repeated, tapping again. *These. These.*

"But they're not even in bloom. They're just buds."

His mother beat the bed with her fist. Patrick's eyes rounded. She hadn't struck him, but he'd never seen her so much as raise a hand to anyone or anything, not even against a buzzing housefly. He'd never seen her angry. Only his father ever landed a blow against him. Once long ago, when he was first learning a shepherd's duties, he let a sheep fall into a ravine, and rather than hauling it out on his own, he'd come to his father, sobbing and shame-faced.

His answer came wrapped in a fist—with an order to finish the job himself.

"You tell me, then," he demanded. "What kind of bride will these bring?"

His mother let her shoulders drop. She took the flowers from him and rustled them in her hand. *These.* She tapped her lips, pressed tight together as always. *Will tell her.* Her forefinger jabbed her son in the breast-bone. *What kind of man you are.*

She laid the bouquet, for that's what it truly was, beside the honey. Her hand stole up onto her son's knee, squeezing it gently. *Trust me. If only because you love me.*

Patrick furrowed his brow. "If you'll let me go back to sleep, I'll promise to bring both with me. I'll let my bride choose which she likes best of them, if I can call one down at all."

His mother stared at him a long time, the expression of her dark eyes unchanging and inscrutable. But finally she nodded, placing both the honey and the bouquet into her son's lap. Then she turned her attention to a few other items spilling from Patrick's rucksack. She prodded them with her hands, occasionally picking one up and inspecting it, nodding approvingly. But one she would not touch. She slapped the blanket near it, glaring in the dark at Patrick.

"Mother—I can't leave that behind. Think about Father's eye."

Her fist curled again, but she only tucked it in her lap this time.

With a downward tilt of her chin, she said, *You won't need it.*

"If I don't need it," Patrick answered stubbornly, "I won't use it."

She opened her mouth—it flapped open and closed, strain showing on her face. She gestured in front of the opening as though she could beckon the sounds out, but eventually she had to give it up. Instead, she leaned forward, pulling her son into a sudden embrace.

Surprised, he returned the gesture, feeling her lips against his cheek, still moving as though she would speak after all. All throughout his childhood, she had been endlessly affectionate toward him. But once he'd turned sixteen, once his father had taken him truly under his wing and begun to teach him about the world, she had withdrawn. So this moment was a shock indeed. He no longer felt like a man. He felt like a small boy again, safe in her arms, in her comforting, familiar silence.

Finally, she broke away from him, gesturing one final time to the bouquet lying on its side to his left. Then she pressed her palm to her heart.

I'm so proud of you, this said. *I'm so happy for us.*

Then she took the chair away from in front of the door, and slunk silently away.

Patrick gathered his travel provisions again, stuffing them back into his rucksack. Only the bouquet he left free on his nightstand, fearful it would be crushed otherwise. A faint sweet smell wafted up from the bundle of stems and grasses. It was a sharper scent than the honey, but less direct somehow, less obvious—as though something lay concealed within it. Patrick picked up the flowers again and held them under his nose, but they refused to give up their secrets.

He extinguished the lamp and lay himself down

again, staring hard into the darkness overhead. He tried to think of tomorrow, of the long climb ahead of him, up the mountain. He tried to think of the bride he would lure down—with whatever gift he chose to offer. But unease nagged him, toying with his thoughts like a cat with a scurrying mouse. He recalled the sensation of his mother's lips against his cheek, mouthing words that were not really words at all. He wondered in his heart what her voice might have sounded like before, all those long years ago, when she still could speak.

He wondered who she might have been, before words were torn from her forever.

CHAPTER 4

A WORD OF CAUTION

IN THE MORNING, Old Matthew's knock woke him. Patrick groaned and staggered from bed, then shrugged quickly into fresh clothes and checked his rucksack. Everything was where it ought to be. He lingered when his eyes fell on his mother's bouquet, the buds still shut like closed lips, half-meaning to stuff it in his top drawer before he departed. But he couldn't make himself leave her gift behind. So he shouldered his pack and met his father at his bedroom door, the bundle of flowers in hand.

Old Matthew cast a leery eye downward. "What's that you've got?"

"They're from—" Patrick started to say. Then something stopped the words in his throat.

He coughed into his fist and began again. "They're for luck. That's all."

His father tugged his rust-colored beard warily. "Luck's no part of this," he told his son. "But have it your way. You're a man now. Have you got everything else you need?"

Patrick patted the rucksack. Old Matthew had instructed him precisely on its contents, on what supplies were necessary for this undertaking. He'd even inspected each item itself, just as carefully as Patrick's mother the night before.

Your gift, he'd told Patrick. *To lure down the wife you want.*

Your net—weighted and balanced, to make her stay.

Your ring if she'll have you.

Your dagger if she won't.

This last, Old Matthew had told him, was the most vital provision of all. Fingering the lambskin patch over his left eye, he said:

"There's nothing in this whole wild world more dangerous to a man than a rebellious bride. I was careless in my youth. You'd do well to learn from my foolishness."

It was a tale Patrick had heard hundreds upon hundreds of times, growing up. And now, as they crept through the solemn halls of Old Matthew's house to the porch door, he was hearing it once more. About how gentle, how *tender* his father had been when his own bride first appeared before him. About how, awestruck by her beauty, he had thrown aside his dagger and his caution and approached her unarmed. How when he finally descended the mountain with Patrick's mother in his arms, his ruined eye continued to weep red tears for many days after.

Patrick had often searched his mother's face, looking for any sign of that old ferocity. But all she would do was smile at him knowingly when she caught him staring. *What do you see when you look at me?* she would say, though her mouth never moved.

Patrick had never been able to answer this. Now he and his father stood on the back porch, staring up towards the mountain's spire in the high, hazy distance. Old Matthew's burning gaze lay steadily against him, and almost too late, Patrick realized he was meant to speak.

"I have what I need," he said.

Old Matthew grunted. "Good. Then you'd better be off—it's a long way up. The other men are sleeping off hangovers, but they'll be ready again to welcome you on your return."

Patrick nodded his thanks and stepped forward, but a firm hand on his rucksack's top loop stopped him in his tracks. He turned to find Old Matthew studying him warily. Any other day, such a look might have set him writing like a spider inside a gas lamp. But today, he met his father's gaze directly. It was then he realized it: in the last year, he'd grown nearly as tall as the old man. Maybe it was because his father had stooped slightly with age, or maybe it was the difference in the slope they stood on.

It was only a disparity of an inch or so—but there it was, just the same.

"Will you really do it, then?" Old Matthew murmured. "I'm not so sure. A wife's different from a wolf. A wolf has only his animal cunning. A bride is a cleverer creature. She can trick you with her words until she's given up her voice. She can gut you with her claws —" Here, his father drew a line from his son's navel to the base of his throat with a stout forefinger. "Or open your veins with her teeth. Learn this well, my son. Until your ring's on her finger, all her promises and flirtations mean nothing. Do you understand me?"

Patrick hesitated, his teeth worrying along his lower lip. His feelings flashed unbidden to his mother again, how her eyes had blazed with hatred at the sight of the dagger lying among his other supplies.

Old Matthew sighed. He cast his cyclopean gaze up the hillside; scattered there across the rippling green was the flock, like a field of bobbing white-headed dandelions.

"When you became a shepherd," he said, "do you remember what I said to you?"

"You've told me so much," Patrick replied automatically.

His father chuckled. "That's the right answer. All right, I'll end the suspense. You asked me how the sheep knew to line up for shearing, why they waited so patiently for it."

Patrick wet his lips. "You told me they only struggle the first time."

"A ewe's wool never stops growing," Old Matthew said with a thin smile. "Soon it covers their eyes, and they can't see to find food or water. Eventually, it becomes too heavy for them to even walk under its weight. They'd starve or smother—and that's wasteful, meaningless suffering. But they can't shear themselves, can they? They need us to do it for them. A man's hands, and a man's kindness. Once they know you mean them no harm and you're giving them relief from their burden, they never forget it. They come to love you for it."

His father looked sidelong at him. "Do you see what I'm telling you?"

Patrick watched the sheep flow slowly across the pasture. He saw Rowan's dark blocky form among them, motionless against the featureless landscape, like a rock standing against the tide. The sheep bunched around his cousin, pressing their wet snouts into his hands and nibbling his pockets, searching for a slice of apple or a handful of oats.

"A man does what he must," Patrick said at last.

Old Matthew's smile broadened. He patted his son's shoulder, then gave him a harder swat on the hindquarters. "Of course you understand it," he gloated. "You're my son."

CHAPTER 5

ARGUMENT WITH A GHOST

THE AIR THINNED ONLY a few hours into the journey.

At first, the walking was easy. He'd passed the pasture, exchanging words with Rowan and receiving bleats of salutation from the ewes when they heard his voice and caught his scent on the wind. And even beyond that, the trail had been simple to follow. It was like a deer path through a forest, the grasses and mosses of the field worn down to the dirt beneath by hundreds of sturdy Blackfrye boots.

But soon the slopes ahead grew steeper, the way forward rockier. Patrick found himself shimmying up and down boulder after black boulder until he was finally only going up. When he looked back, the world seemed to drop away beneath him. Blackfrye looked like a faraway painting of a village, its lights and houses cast in grotesque miniature. He pressed himself flat against the slope, his hands sweating on their holds on the rock, his heart knocking against the door of his ribs. From that moment on, he would only look up.

He paused often in the climb, but never for more than a few short moments. The higher he rose, the colder the air grew. Cold was treacherous—it could seep into his muscles, stiffen him like hide left on a pasture fence in the summertime. His legs might betray him. His fingers might curl like claws and lose their grip. It was a long way down if he slipped, and then his only bride would be the scavengers that came to pick his flesh over, and the worms and maggots after that.

Patrick only truly rested once, just after the sun reached its zenith in the sky. The air had grown hazy now, and moisture kissed his cheeks with every breath of the wind. He'd risen so high that the gray clouds had crept in around him, a wet smothering embrace that slicked his hair and coated the insides of his lungs. Patrick found a cliff wide enough to park his weight and sat cross-legged, his rucksack lumped beside him. He took his lunch out and ate slowly—a half-loaf, a wedge of cheese, and a few slices of salted mutton. The bread he sliced with the dagger and spread a little of the honey on it, watching as far below him, the afternoon sun burned mist off the black rocks.

A little rain passed through, and Patrick took shelter under his father's cloak, making a tent with his arms. Then he shook himself dry and continued the climb.

When dusk came, he hardly noticed at first. His gaze was fixed upward, and the sky stayed light while the advancing shadow of the great peak slowly swallowed the valley behind him. But soon the mountain began to deceive him. A sure handhold became a loose stone that pried loose in his grip; a foothold was really only a shadow on the cliff-face. His hands sweated, and his eyes stung. Every breath seemed to bruise his lungs. And the wind had grown claws, pulling his cloak away from his body like a sail, tugging him closer and closer to the long, screaming drop. But he clung fast to the mountain's bosom, fighting for inches, letting the darkening sky beckon him upward.

And finally, *finally*—the cliffs became slopes again, and then leveled off flat. Patrick stumbled to his feet, struggling out of his rucksack's straps and hurling it to the ground. He stood under the spreading palm of the night with his head between his knees, sucking breath after shaky breath. Every joint in his body ached; his muscles felt ready to slide off their bones like meat left spinning too long over a fire.

But he couldn't rest. Dusk had become true night, and the few speckling stars that had watched over the last leg of his climb had called their sisters to their sides. Patrick's eyes darted across the sky, scanning nervously for movement. Only when he saw that he was alone did he reach for his pack again. He unclasped the top flap and carefully unfolded the sturdy woven net so it wouldn't tangle. It had been his father's, and his father's before him, in a long line stretching back before memory could claim. The webbing was strong but soft to the touch and would not chafe when wrapped across tender skin. The iron weights fastened along the edges clacked together like teeth.

It was old but strong, like the hands that wove it. It had caught many brides.

Patrick weighed it in his hands, stretching its stitches, testing its joinings. Then, when he was satisfied, he put it aside and began to prepare in earnest.

The mountain's peak was not so broad. From where he'd crested the summit to where it fell away again was barely the span of the greatroom of Old Matthew's house. Twenty paces to Patrick's left, a cluster of jagged boulders broke through the rocky soil, each half again as tall as himself. He'd heard stories of course—from Rowan, from other Blackfrye husbands, even from his own father—of long hours spent crouching among those same rocks, waiting for a bride to reveal herself.

"It'll be easy getting down on one knee when the

time comes, cousin," Rowan had joked to him once. "Standing back up again—now that's the trick."

Toward the center of the summit stood a less natural formation. A stack of stones, each about as wide and flat as a dinner plate, formed a kind of altarpiece, reaching as high as Patrick's waist. He strode toward it, examining it from every angle. Countless gifts had been laid on this smooth gray rock; countless Blackfrye men had fallen prostrate here, begging for the one thing they could not get for themselves by their cunning or the strength of their arms alone. Patrick hefted his rucksack, feeling inside for the honey pot. A little sweet nectar was left around the lid and stuck to his fingers when he fished it out. It hadn't come cheaply. Honey had to be imported from the hives in Wicke, and transporting it had cost Patrick nearly a month's pay.

But it was worth it. The taste was sweeter than anything he'd sampled in his life, and the temptation to simply gobble it up himself had vexed him for months.

It would lure a fine wife indeed.

A sweet wife—like he'd told the other men he wanted. *And yet...*

And yet his mother's face swam into his thoughts. It was like she stood beside him on that dark mountain peak. Patrick felt the prickle of her stare, the terrible pressure of her focus. He saw her eyes, black as stones, flashing out of every star that spun overhead in its course across the heavens, imploring him because her mouth could not.

Do this for me. If only because you love me.

"It's still my choice," Patrick reasoned. "She isn't here to see. Why couldn't I merely tell her I left the flowers, if it would make her so happy?"

If only because you love me.

"I'll still give your offering after," Patrick vowed—aloud, though there was truly nobody there to hear it but himself. "A second gift, for accepting my proposal..."

If only because you love me.

"Who are you to order me around?" he snarled aloud. "Maybe that was all right before, when I was small, hiding behind your skirts. But I'm grown now, and I'm a man. I don't care what you want. I don't want anything to do with you."

This prompted no reply. His mother's face fled his thoughts. His cheeks burning with indignation, he turned to go, leaving the honey pot left open on the stone platform. But he only got a few paces away before he paused, wrestling with himself. He swore a foul oath that stung the stars and marched straight back to the altar.

When he returned to the boulders, his rucksack was on his back, and the honey jar dangled from his fist, bumping against his hip. He threw the pack into the center of the boulders, then climbed after it—not a moment too soon. The instant he had crouched out of sight, a furtive shadow darted beneath the blanket of stars. One by one, frantic shapes whistled across the sky; powerful, leathered wings smote the air. One screeching voice called out across the vast night, followed by another, and again another, then dozens, hundreds more.

Patrick's breath purled in his lungs. He licked his fingers, hardly tasting the honey's cloying sweetness. All around him, the air churned and battered. The stars flickered, then snuffed out, leaving only blackness in their stead. It was happening—it was happening at last.

The brides, in their multitudes, had come down from the heavenly dark.

CHAPTER 6

NIGHT COMES DOWN THE MOUNTAIN

WHAT A MARVEL A STORM of harpies was, streaming out of the night.

Patrick had seen one before, of course. But she had been alone, and quite a long distance up—half a mile at least, soaring just below the clouds in the pre-dawn light. He remembered seeing her shadow first, surging across the grass like it was being jerked along at the end of a string. Thinking it was some great bird of prey, he'd looked up and been momentarily blinded as his gaze swung crazily into the sunrise. Only when his vision stopped dancing did he spot her at last, for the briefest instant. A wingtip, a hoary head, a pale face tilted up at the sun. Then she rose like a kite on the wind, folding up into the high gray clouds.

Now hundreds circled him. They were so numerous that their passage changed the course of the wind, their breath boiled the very air in his lungs. The night was full of their grim and terrible splendor, and Patrick felt his senses desert him. He simply watched as the brides surged and squalled, bespelled by their grace and fury.

Only at first glance did they resemble anything human. Their bodies were dark and slender and shaped much like his own, but as Patrick watched them dance across the night sky, he realized their clothes were not linen or silk but their own dusky pelts, smooth as buttermilk to cut through the air. Their legs were humanlike but ended in claws like a hawk's, and between them hung denser fur in a concealing tuft. And from their shoulders, where there should be arms, sprouted the wings of immense bats. Their bony fingers spread impossibly wide, and between their span quivered blood-pink, veiny membranes, thin as a bedsheet. These too ended in curving claws, shorter and more delicate-looking than the graspers on their feet, but no less fearsome.

Even their countenances were not truly human. Raven-haired and stone-eyed, with thin, hungry faces and dark mouths whose tempting lips were the exact shade of dried blood. The ears were also batlike, swept back along their heads, and as long as butcher knives. But nothing under the heavens could subtract from the charisma of those faces. Their eyes constantly darted, and their hair whipped and frenzied as they wheeled and dipped, mocking the earth below with their flight.

They were like the wives of Blackfrye, and yet they were much more as well.

Wilder, sharper. Dangerous as the red glow of a stove, and just as alluring.

But they were all lovely—so very beautiful, in fact, that it struck Patrick as absurd that a creature such as these might actually become his bride. But it must be so. Not a fate but a duty, and his to fulfil. He had the net laid beside him now, ready. He reached down slowly to finger its weave, then slipped his hand into his pocket to touch the smooth metal of the ring. The dagger hung from a sheath on his belt now, resting against his hip. He felt a twinge of guilt even thinking about it, imagining again his mother's solemn judgment at the sight of it.

Then he thought of his father's ruined eye, and the warning of its dead glance. It brought him no warmth or comfort, but it steeled his nerves enough to swallow away his guilt.

A man does what he must.

He inched farther up the rock, peering closer at the flocking brides. The main body of the screeching multitude stayed well away from the mountain peak as though it were a candle's flame, too hot to touch. But now he noticed one lone harpy dipping lower, diving nearer—*she was circling the altar*, he realized with a racing kind of thrill. She was inspecting his mother's bouquet. And as she drew closer and closer, the cawing and shrieking of her sisters grew ever-louder. Patrick held his breath. The harpy swooped lower; she fluttered, she hovered. For a single beat of a heart, she seemed to hang motionless in the night air...

Then, she dropped suddenly to the earth, landing on all fours beside the stones.

Movement exploded all around him. Like startled fish in a stream, the brides scattered, breaking up their formation and flashing away in every direction at once. It was like blowing out a lantern. They were there—then with a hiss and a beat of leathery wings, they seemed to melt into the darkness. The stars returned. The tumult of the wind ceased. Now there was no sound at all but a dull, distant beating. It was his own heart, keeping anxious time within him. Only the harpy on the ground remained, hunched double like a hag, hobbling on wing-tips that seemed ill-suited for such clumsy use. Patrick watched as she tipped her velvet head back, her mouth yawning open to deliver one final screech of farewell to her sisters. Then she crept toward the tower of smooth stones, toward the bouquet her husband-to-be left just for her.

Patrick wished he were closer. He wished with all

his strength she would turn her face toward him, only slightly. He prayed for a glimpse of her features, hidden now by the wild tangle of her windblown hair—for a glance, even the ghost of a smile.

Instead, she gifted him with an even more magical sight.

The harpy straightened, tottering for a moment on only her back claws, folding her lustrous black wings around herself. Then she began to change. The hunch of her shoulders smoothed away. The long drape of her wings shrank upward until they became a heavy black fur cloak, beneath which slender shoulders jumped and shrugged. Now bare human feet wiggled their toes in the hard dirt of the mountaintop, and smooth hairless legs stood erect before the stone altar. And from beneath the cloak, one small white hand reached carefully forward and plucked the bouquet from its perch.

Then came the second wonder. Moonlight struck the closed buds of the bouquet, hidden among the long pale grasses. The light seemed to cut their seams, and they burst open, delivering into the world furling white blooms that seemed to glow of their own accord, or at least reflect the moon's radiance up into the darkness. Patrick heard the harpy gasp. She buried her nose among the blossoms and breathed deep of their strange, sweet scent. She stood quivering before the altar a moment, then two. Then she clutched the bouquet to her bosom, tipped back her head to the moon-filled sky, and laughed.

The sound stopped Patrick's heart in its paces. It would stop clocks, he was certain, or even halt a river in its course. No Blackfrye wife had ever made a sound like that. What wouldn't he give to hear it again? What wouldn't he do to be the cause of that laughter, to set that kind of joy springing in that trembling breast? But these were fleeting thoughts. His task was not yet over. He'd lured his bride to earth. Now he had to marshal up all his strength and wits—else his long and dangerous journey would be for nothing.

He briefly shut his eyes, tracing a blessing against his chest with trembling fingers. Then he reached for the net and lifted it slowly, willing his heart *still, still, still...*

A sudden rush, a terrible clatter of loose stones—he was too hasty leaping clear of the rocks that concealed him from sight. His bride twisted toward him, dark eyes flashing, mouth dropping open to reveal rows of frightening yellow fangs, her cloak spreading wide to catch the wind. But she was not swift enough. He swept his arm forward and hurled the net. It spun open, stretching wide like a grasping palm. It struck her heavily, the iron weights wrapping tight around her body, crushing her to the earth. She rolled away, screeching. Patrick pursued, his hand finding by instinct the hilt of the dagger at his belt.

Finally, she slowed, ending up face-down in the dirt, the net cinched so tight around her thrashing form that her cloak pushed in diamonds through the webbing. She jerked in its grasp, but nothing could free her. Soon, she seemed to tire and lay gasping on the ground, groaning and shrieking equally when she could catch breath. Patrick crept nearer on anxious feet. She was close enough to touch now. With one hand, he felt in his pocket for the ring. With the other, he stretched out and took her by the shoulder.

She startled at his touch, twisting suddenly toward him. Her hair flew back from her face, and in that moment, Patrick stared into the eyes of his new bride at last.

CHAPTER 7

THE BRIDE YOU WANT

"I'LL KILL YOU," she said.

It made him jump back. The words were warning enough, but what truly unraveled him was the sound of her voice. Patrick hadn't ever heard a noise like it before. Once, Rowan had nursed a raven's chick who'd lost its nest, and this creature could croak a few hoarse syllables —but it was hardly the same. The harpy's voice rasped, but it was still a human voice, with a strange trembling softness under its wrath, like snow beneath ice.

When her red lips moved and twisted, Patrick saw the points of many tiny teeth, all yellow like wheat and all very sharp.

"I'll kill you," the harpy repeated. "I've got teeth, and I've got claws. I'll spill out your insides on that altar there and lick up the blood—and I'll like it."

Patrick quickly spread his hands before him. "I...I don't mean any harm."

It was, of course, the truth. But the hesitation in his voice rang each word false. He wasn't certain what tone he should take—whether he should be bold or contrite, flash or common. He'd had no practice, and he'd never spoken so much as a word to any of the wives of Blackfrye save for his own mother. Even this was in secret, and she never talked back.

She certainly never threatened to tear out his throat.

"He doesn't mean any harm," the harpy mocked, her eyes round and rolling. "I see that dagger stuck in your belt. That's for picking your teeth, is it?"

Patrick flushed with shame. Cheeks burning, he tugged his cloak forward so it covered up the dangling sheath. The harpy lurched and flopped in the net's grip, managing to sit up and face him at last. Her dark eyes were deep pits of hate, glistening at the far corners. Her mouth hung open, panting, and beneath her cloak her bosom heaved out and in. Patrick couldn't help but stare. Other than the fur wrapped snug around her torso, she wasn't wearing a stitch of clothes.

"I wasn't going to use it," he protested, reddening deeper still.

"Oh, yes, you were," the harpy fired back. "I've

heard that line before. And I know men's promises aren't worth the breath they cost. Look here..."

She whipped her head around so her hair fell away from one ear. Patrick suppressed a gasp. The upper lobe had a deep slash in it, red and angry, like a vulture's open, bloody beak. The wound had healed closed, but only just—it looked like a touch or a strong wind might undo the seam again. Seeing his expression, the harpy grinned scornfully.

"Lost your nerve?" she scolded. "Am I not beautiful enough for you now?"

Again, Patrick found himself struck mute. And again, he saw his mother's eyes burning at the sight of the dagger. Guilt twisted inside him like an animal in a trap. When his hands moved to the belt, it was without his willing it. The harpy flinched backward, hissing and baring her yellow teeth. But Patrick didn't draw the weapon. Instead, he unfastened the buckle, moved a few paces away, and laid the whole apparatus at the base of the altar.

Then he returned to his bride, heart thudding, empty hands upraised.

"I...I think you're very beautiful," he said.

The harpy stared at him. Her eyes still smoldered, but the hatred there was coals now instead of bonfires.

She moistened her lips, pressing them together in a tight line.

"Well," she said slowly. "That's sweet of you. I'll still tear your lungs out."

"Not like that, you won't." Patrick gestured to the net, to the harpy's pinioned arms.

"Oh, no?" She rocked back and forth, wriggling, but the net held stubbornly fast. "I don't suppose you'd untangle me?" she asked, batting her eyes contemptuously.

Patrick knotted his hands. "I like my insides where they are."

"Then we're at loggerheads," replied the harpy. "It's like this. Either you let me free and let me rip you from there to there—" With her eyes, she indicated Patrick's midsection, then the hollow of his throat. "—or you leave me here trapped, and I die of thirst or starve."

This wasn't right, he thought to himself. None of this was going how it should. He didn't like the way the harpy looked at him, with her black eyes and red mocking mouth. He didn't like how she twisted his words back around. They came back sharper, barbed like a fishhook. And he hated most of all the weak, clammy way her presence made him feel. It wasn't just fatigue after the long climb. He felt ill—reduced somehow, eaten away inside. If she asked him again to free her, he worried he wouldn't be able to refuse.

"Come back with me, then," Patrick said helplessly. "You could just say yes."

The harpy sneered. "How very romantic."

But though her tone remained mocking as before, her expression was split between two moods. She tilted her nose toward the sky, her eyes half-lidded and fluttering.

"Come closer," she ordered.

When Patrick dithered, the harpy rolled her eyes toward the high moon. "I can't hurt you tangled up like this. You said so yourself. I just want your scent—is that so frightening to you?"

Chastened, Patrick edged closer. The harpy watched his approach warily, keeping her eyes trained carefully on his outstretched hands. He kept them spread open in what he hoped was a gesture of peace. At last, he was near enough to touch her and, feeling more than a little foolish, stretched one arm out in her direction.

"What are you—" he began to say.

The harpy twisted forward faster than he could think. Patrick flinched and squeezed his eyes shut—but he didn't feel her teeth. Instead, she ran her narrow, pointed nose up and down the length of his arm, sniffing and making small squeaking noises in her throat.

Finally, her eyes sprang wide. "You. You're Fay's child?"

Patrick drew his arm away, every small hair tickling. "I'm not sure what you mean."

"You don't know your own mother's name?" The harpy scoffed.

Then she frowned and seemed to reconsider. "No. No, I suppose you couldn't."

"How do you know who my mother is?" Patrick demanded, and the harpy grinned slyly.

"I can smell her milk on your breath," she told him.

Patrick made a face. "I haven't nursed in eighteen years. I'm not an infant."

"That's not such a long time to a harpy." She shrugged—then her face tilted toward him again, measuring him with her gaze. "The White Ladies. They weren't your idea?"

"The flowers?" Patrick's cheeks burned with new embarrassment. But he couldn't deny it. She'd know somehow if he did, this creature who knew the scent of his mother's milk—who knew his mother, even from so long ago.

"She gave them to me," he admitted. "Did...do you like them?"

"I'm here, aren't I?" the harpy muttered.

But her mind seemed far afield. She stared sideways into the darkness, watching one star wink on, then off, then on again, like a slow-blinking eye. She was silent for so long it was like she'd forgotten Patrick was there at all.

"Listen," she said at last, without looking at him. "Fay's son. What's your name?"

Patrick told her. The harpy nodded as if this confirmed some riddle she'd been puzzling over. She seemed to be wrestling with something in her head; she seemed to be losing.

At last, she spoke again: "All right, Patrick. I think perhaps we can help each other."

"How's that?" Patrick asked.

Her eyes cut toward him, then back out at the night. "You might not know this," she began, "or you might not care at all. But Fay, your mother—she was a great lady in her day, among harpies. And I owe her a debt, something I can't leave unsettled."

Patrick stayed perfectly still. The atmosphere on the mountaintop had changed. The air was thinner now than before, like the dark itself was holding its breath.

"What kind of debt?" The words left his lips in a whisper.

"That's my affair," the harpy snapped.

"Oh..."

"But then again," she went on, "I can't go to Black-frye alone, can I?"

Again, she seemed to struggle against something inside, her sharp little jaw working like she'd saw through her own tongue with her teeth. Patrick watched her carefully, holding his breath. The harpy watched the night roll past, or nothing at all.

"If you take me back..." she began.

"Yes...?"

"*If you take me back*," she cut him off with a snap of her sharp teeth. "If you let me talk with your mother—alone. Then I'll...I'll do it. I'll give you what you came here for. I'll wear your wedding band and give up my wings for you. I'll be the bride you want."

For a long moment, it was like Patrick hadn't heard. Then he was digging fiercely inside his pocket, the ring dodging his clumsy fingers again and again.

A hard glare from the harpy quelled his frenzy.

"There are conditions to this," she hissed at him. "If I'm going to settle my business with Fay, I've actually got to speak with her. That means I've got to keep my voice, and that means I've got to keep my wings, at least for a little while longer."

Patrick had fished the ring out at last, but now he paused. "You'll just fly away."

The harpy shook her head. "I won't. Not if we travel in the daytime. No harpy can change her shape under sunlight. You should know that—you're half harpy yourself."

Patrick snorted in spite of himself. "There are no male harpies. Everyone knows that."

"Suit yourself." She turned a haughty face away from him. "I suppose you know it all, then. I was clearly mistaken—you're a man all over, right down to your boots."

Patrick wrinkled his nose, his father's instructions ringing in his ears. "You're trying to trick me. I should just take your wings now and be done with it."

"*No...!*"

It flew from the harpy's lips in a screech. She kicked the stony ground, slithering a few feet back in spite of her bindings. "I mean to say..." she panted, "I'm going to be your wife. A husband and wife should learn to trust each other, shouldn't they?"

Your wife. The words chimed in his brain like a spell. He wondered if there might really be some magic afoot in that place; he felt so strange in this creature's presence. But all this fell into the pit in the back of his mind the longer he looked upon her.

She *was* beautiful.

She was beautiful, and she was *his*.

"I agree to this," he said. "You have my word."

"That's not enough," the harpy replied. "Swear it on her. On your mother."

Patrick swore it again. The harpy grimaced like she'd swallowed something vile. But she said, "Then you have my word as well, Fay's son."

He approached, less cautiously now, with a bound in his step. The ring lay cradled in the palm of his hand. The harpy quailed back reflexively as he drew close.

"Take off the net at least," she begged. "Let's do this properly."

Patrick knelt at her side. He felt foolish, trembling as he did. He was still cautious around her teeth. But the harpy stayed still as he unwound the silken net from her body, only quivering every so often when his fingers would brush against her heavy cloak. The fur seemed to bristle at his touch, though this could just be his imagination.

Then at last her bonds lay heaped on the rocks. He offered a hand, and she slipped hers into his grasp, letting herself be helped up to her feet. It was warm, this simple touch, and her skin was soft as lamb's wool— shivers trickled through him every time her fingers flexed against his palm. She stared at their twined hands as though bewitched, like her eyes were playing tricks.

"I'm shaking," was all she could say.

"Don't be scared," he urged. "I'll be a good husband to you."

The harpy cast her eyes down. "Of course you will."

"What's your name?" he asked her.

The harpy smirked in spite of herself. "Finally, he thinks to ask. I'm called Stella."

Patrick nodded. Blood coursed in his ears. He tried to remember his speech, his pretty, prepared words. But in the end, simplicity won the day. He clasped the harpy's hand, turning it palm down. Carefully, he slipped the metal band onto the correct finger.

A perfect fit. He tried to keep his voice level, to keep his own hand from shaking.

"Stella," he said, "will you come back to Blackfrye with me? Will you be my bride?"

The harpy searched Patrick's face. He wished someday she'd find whatever she was looking for there. He wished it hard. Slowly, she drew her hand free and gazed at the ring under the strong moonlight, twisting it this way and that, observing every angle.

"I'll do what I must," she whispered, like he wasn't there at all.

My son...

Although you do not know it yet, I've sent you into the lion's den, the very jaws of the beast. You think you've won a bride, and perhaps you have, but the true prize I fear may be mine alone. I hope you'll forgive my deception and my desperation.

And I hope your sweet temper and your love for me will survive all my terrible treachery. I loved you for eighteen wonderful years. I was his for eighteen years of torment and silence. Now love and grief must die together.

Now your mother must seize something of her own.

CHAPTER 8
A SHOWING OF WOUNDS

THE CAVERN WAS long and dusky, and along its dripping ceiling roosted score after score of dangling bats. They fluttered and screamed as Patrick walked beneath them, but wouldn't descend from their perches. One wore Stella's face like it was a large wooden mask; another wore his mother's. A third peered down at him through his father's single, lifeless eyehole, twisting its head around to fix him directly with its gaze.

"I'll kill you," it squeaked, its voice muffled by the mask. "I'll tear your lungs out."

These were Stella's words, not his father's. But this difference didn't seem to matter in the cave. The lambskin patch peeled away, and Patrick found himself gazing up into the red terror of Old Matthew's ruined left eye, pulpy cords of tissue dangling like moss. The other bats erupted in flight, jigging around the bat that was his father. They began to tear at those bloody strands with their teeth, swarming until there were so many that Old Matthew disappeared under the smother of their velvety wings.

Patrick couldn't move, even when his father's voice boomed above the squall.

"The dagger!" he screamed. "Patrick—help me!"

Slowly, slowly—his hand groped blindly for his belt. But it wasn't the rough twine of the dagger's hilt that met his fumbling touch. It was something soft, something warm.

Soft warm fingers, with tips sharp as daggers, threading between his own...

His eyes flew open; his heart thrashed like prey in a cage. Morning was near, and low cool sun slid needles under his eyelids. He looked about for Stella, feeling behind him on the rumpled cloak he'd spread beneath them the night before.

But the space was empty and cold.

The rush of dread in his chest was short-lived, however. He found her perched only a few paces away, crouched on the boulders where he'd hidden the evening past. Her wings hugged close around her body, and her long claws dug into the black stone beneath her. She stared down over the long drop, down toward Blackfrye, still and quiet as though she were carved from the rock, her dark eyes hidden under the wild, wind-tossed banner of her dark hair.

Only when he got to his feet did she look his way. Her red lips were pressed together, and her eyes, which had flashed so brightly under the moonlight, held no expression now. Slowly and rather clumsily, she slipped off the rocks, sliding out of her harpy shape like an arm slipping from a shirt sleeve. Once more, her wings were a full-length fur cloak. Once more, her bare toes dug in the rocky mountain dirt.

Patrick could only stare.

"You were tossing in your sleep," she muttered, and turned back to the panorama.

They ate a picnic breakfast on the mountaintop. Stella's appetite had no bottom. The remaining bread and cheese held no interest for her, but the salted mutton vanished just as fast as she could get her hands on it. She licked her fingers clean, ignoring the rust-colored juice that trickled down her chin. She hardly looked at Patrick, keeping her gaze fixed on the thin gray smoke that rose from the village in the distance.

Patrick thought of a hundred silent evenings, his mother and father staring at each other across the long oak dinner table by flickering candlelight. A knot twisted his belly—like hunger, but not really hunger, something more, some terrible nameless want.

Then they started their descent. The climb down didn't loosen Stella's tongue. Her long white limbs, so graceful in flight before, now scrabbled and slipped on the black stones of the dizzying mountain slopes. And she kept clutching at her cloak, fighting to keep her body covered as wind gusts tried to claw it off her back. She rebuffed all Patrick's efforts to assist her, as well as any attempt at conversation.

Finally, he could stand it no longer.

"Haven't you got anything to say to me?" he asked her.

Her darkened countenance twisted toward him as she fought her way down one moss-covered boulder. "Marriage," she grunted, "is a quiet game. I'm getting into practice."

Patrick's face grew hot. "I haven't taken your wings yet."

"I'm wearing your ring." She thrust out one glittering hand. "You want me to talk, too?"

With only one hand bracing on the rock, Stella lost her grip, landing in a heap of knees and elbows at Patrick's feet. She smote the boulder with her fist, growling deep in her throat. He stood over her help-lessly, folding and unfolding his arms over and over.

"You know," he said sheepishly, "some Blackfrye men carry their brides home."

Her red lips bent into a snarl. "You think I'll let you carry me?"

Stella swatted his offered hand away and rose to her full height, yellowed fangs flashing in his face. She was slender, but hardly shorter than Patrick.

Defeated, he shook his head. "No, I suppose you won't."

She brushed past him to the next sloping rock. "Then what's there to talk about?"

Patrick pursued her. "I've offended you."

"No," she snarled. "You've been a *gentleman*."

"But you're angry. Tell me what I've done."

She had descended ahead of him a little, halfway down the next mossy drop. But now she scrambled back to his level again with surprising quickness, storming up so close to him he could smell the salted mutton still on her breath.

"Fay's son or no, you won't trick me. Not with words. Not with this...*false courtesy*. I know what's waiting for me in that valley. You won't make me forget."

"What's waiting?" Patrick repeated. "Family, you mean. Children. Happy-afters."

Stella gave an awful snort. "I like the way you talk. When you hold your face like that, I can almost imagine you really believe what you're saying."

Patrick felt his cheeks boil as his hands curled into knots. "How can you talk like that?" he demanded, louder than he meant to. "What could you know about it?"

"What could I know?" Stella's brows raised. Her red mocking mouth sneered hideously, showing every yellow jagged tooth. "What could I know? I know what happy-after means to men like you. I know what you want. You want *brides*."

She said this last word like a curse, like it would sting his ears or sear his skin. For one horrible second, Patrick thought she would lash out with her claws—or worse, laugh at him, or simply hurl herself down the stupefying drop. But she didn't.

She only talked, but by the end, it was like she'd struck him all the same.

"This was years ago..." she began. "Many years, likely before you were even born. Another man came to that mountaintop. A young man, like you, with his gift laid out on those same stacked stones. His mother didn't advise him to bring a bride flowers, so his gift was a bowl of mutton stew, heated over a fire he'd built among the rocks. I'd never tasted hot food before, but the smell made my mouth water and my stomach cry out greedily. So I dropped down from the sky, in spite of my trepidation. He let me approach, and I ate my fill.

"I didn't see his trap until it was almost too late.

"But he was slower than you, this other man. The net was heavy in his hands. Only one wing got caught; I had my claws still and my fangs. I could have torn him to ribbons. But I'd never seen a man up close before. There are no harpy grooms, after all. I was stupid, letting him come so near. But I listened when he spoke gently, making me pleasing promises. A roof, a family, hot food like that every night for the rest of my life. Do you understand? I wanted to believe him. I wanted it to be true that there was happiness to be found on the earth after all.

"He got down on one knee, just like you. He asked me to be his bride.

"But then his fire rose up and caught his bearded face in full light, and I saw just how those hard eyes gleamed as they danced across my body, still in the net. I saw in them that I'd been tricked, that only want and pain and cruelty waited for me in the valley. I saw that he was cruel, and he meant to use me cruelly.

"And this man—he *saw* that I knew. He saw, and he didn't care.

"So I showed him my fury. He showed me his. We danced among the jagged rocks. He was quicker with his dagger than with his net, and he cut me badly. So badly, in fact, that the wound hasn't ever closed, and I've never been free from the pain since."

One thin pale hand drifted up, pushing away dark hair so Stella's slashed ear gleamed red under the morning sun. The scar was raw and flaking, a puckering horror.

"But I cut him as well," the harpy crowed. "Oh—he bled wonderfully. When I shut my eyes, I can still conjure the smell of it. He won't forget *this* runaway bride so easily. And I'll know him again if our flights cross, by the scar I gave him as a parting gift."

She'd been facing the sun, the dawn melting in a soft halo around her silhouette. Now she turned toward him, fixing Patrick with a hard, searching look.

"I know you don't care about any of that," she concluded. "That's just fine. I made this dread bargain, and I'll honor it—but let that be all. I won't pretend there's more than that between us. I just can't."

Then she turned her face again. She hugged her fur cloak tight to her, like she could squeeze herself into nothing. Patrick leaned hard against the rock slope at his back. Thoughts tumbled like loose stones in his head. Stella's shoulders hunched—a sudden urge struck him to reach out for her, to pull her to him. He fought it down.

Instead, he too began to speak.

"You say you know my mother," he began. "Did you know my grandmother, too?"

Slowly, Stella shook her head. So he went on saying:

"My grandfather...Toby. He's had two brides, not just one. The first was my father's mother—this new one, I suppose, she's not anything to me. But when I was small, I thought my grandmother was my best friend in the whole world. We couldn't talk, of course, but she could scratch shapes in the dirt, or take my hand to show me what she wanted me to see. She was already so old, and she needed help with almost everything, and I could always be on hand to help her with anything she wanted from me. My father didn't like me following her around, but he was busy so often and couldn't shoo me from behind her skirts all the time. And my grandfather didn't care one way or the other."

"The night of my seventh birthday, she appeared in my room like a ghost and crawled into the bed with me. She had shrunk with age so much by then that there was space for both of us, and room to spare. She wrapped her arms around my shoulders and put my hand against her mouth, her lips moving like she was talking. She had a bit of a moustache, and it tickled on my skin. I didn't know why she was there, but eventually she gave it up and fell asleep beside me.

"I only realized later she was saying goodbye."

Stella didn't turn. She had become very still suddenly. Only her heels shifted against the rocks, clicking them together. In a low voice, she asked, "How did it happen?"

Patrick shaded his eyes. "I know what they told me. My father sat me down the morning after and explained that older wives get confused sometimes. He said that she'd gone out to the cliffs sometime before first light with an old tablecloth around her shoulders—like a cloak, you see. She thought she still had her wings. She thought she could still fly..."

He shook his head, fighting against the awful tightness bubbling up his throat. He willed it down, and down again. He forced it away.

"But maybe that wasn't right," he said. "Maybe that's what she wanted us all to think. In the end, maybe she was simply unhappy with us. With me.

"I didn't see my mother for three days after that. She stayed in the bedroom she shared with my father and broke furniture against the walls. I guess a lot of the other Blackfrye wives did the same. My grandfather, he spent that time getting drunk with my father. And I was left all alone. I didn't understand why nobody would speak to me about it. The men, their eyes just sort of slid over me like I wasn't even there. The quiet was like...the air before a thunderstorm. Full of terrible energy, with nowhere at all to go.

"Once in the early morning, I went to the cliffs and looked down, thinking I might see her down there. I was young and stupid, and I thought maybe if we could find her, we could pull her back up, and that everything would be all right. But I didn't even see the tablecloth.

"The next week, three strong men went up the mountain with my grandfather. The next night, they came back down again—with his new young bride carried between them in their arms. And nobody, not even my father, ever talked about my grandmother again."

Now he did reach for Stella. He didn't quite mean to—his hand somehow found her slender wrist, grasping it desperately, like she was the string of a kite that had nearly slipped through his fingers. She whirled at his touch, but didn't pull free. The expression in her wine-dark eyes had no name. A question danced on her red lips, unspoken.

Patrick spoke first. "But *you* won't be unhappy like that," he promised—as though only by saying the words, he could make it real. "I swear, I won't let you. I'll be a good husband to you. I won't let it happen again."

Then he rubbed his eyes at last, with the other hand. Mountain mist had collected on his face; he couldn't seem to get his cheeks dry.

"I'm sorry," he said. "I didn't think I was going to say all that."

"I didn't think you were going to listen," Stella said slowly. But she didn't pull free.

Instead, she leaned forward, watching his face. Her eyes blazed with wrath, and her red lips pressed together in one stony line. But when she finally twisted out of his grip, she didn't pull her hand away. Instead, very carefully, she threaded their fingers together—for one second, then two, then three. The pressure of her grip increased.

Then she pulled free again, and the moment was over.

"I won't promise to be happy," she said. "But...I could do worse than you, I think."

"Now you're making fun," Patrick said. But he dried his eyes and tried to smile.

He could still feel the warmth of her hand against his fingers.

"I want to know something," he told her. "If you're

so frightened of Blackfrye, why not stay clear of the mountain altogether? Why did you come back?"

Now it was Stella's turn to shade her eyes. She gazed down into the valley, where the black jagged rocks fell away gradually into gentler green slopes, with no line where one ended and the other began. The change was smooth as a painter's brush. She stepped carefully off the next rocky ledge, descending without looking back at him.

"Maybe I'll tell you someday," she called back, and that was all.

THE REMAINING descent was quiet again. But the silence between them was somehow easier. Each lull was full of bright birdsong and the distant bleating of the flock flowing across the pasture like oil in a cooking pan. The sun had already burned the clouds off the horizon and now soared steadily closer, warming their skin and shrinking their shadows. The slopes were getting easier, the rocks drier, their footing steadier. It was becoming a lovely day.

As they climbed down, Stella kept catching Patrick's eye. She'd been watchful before, but this wasn't caution anymore. Every time he caught her looking, she'd glance away with a sly expression that left his chest pleasantly tight and his face in flames. She'd wait a few minutes, long enough that it might have been an accident, then do it again.

It was like a game with no rules and no score. Once, Patrick stared until she caught him at it, jerking her gaze away again with red blossoming cheeks.

Soon, the path flattened, then leveled altogether, and Patrick's boots found the foot trail leading back into Blackfrye. The pastures rolled out ahead of them, the clouds' shadows bumbling over the ground in ragged patterns like a patchwork quilt. On the wind—the ewes' mellow chorus, the clank of one rusted iron bell, and Rowan's low voice calling to them, guiding them to heartier grazing.

"That's my cousin," Patrick remarked. "He'll want to meet you right away."

Stella stopped short. Her frame went stiff and hunched beneath her cloak. "I've still got my wings," she murmured, pulling the fur close. "He'll know you didn't..."

She didn't need to say what Patrick hadn't done.

He dropped to his haunches, balancing his chin on folded hands. Soft meadow wind breathed over him. He watched tufts of soft grass move, pressed down by the insistent palm of the breeze. He thought, and thought.

Then he straightened again, wincing as his knees clicked beneath him.

"Will you wait here?" he asked, turning back to Stella.

She eyed him cautiously. "What for?"

"If you stay out of sight," Patrick told her, "I might find you some spare wings."

Stella narrowed her gaze at him. But then, reluctantly, she nodded, stepping back and crouching below the sightline of the nearest low hill. Patrick put a finger to his lips and began to circle the pasture, giving Rowan and the flock a wide berth. The ewes likely had his scent already, but so long as his cousin was at their head, they wouldn't seek him out. Against his chest, he drew a sign for luck with his fingers. He prayed Rowan wouldn't spot him.

He prayed the wolf's carcass still lay where he'd left it.

Slowly, slowly—he circumvented the pasture, moving from bluff to bluff, half-crouching, half-crawling, his cloak dragging in the grass behind him. But at last, the rounded boulder swung into view, and he crept behind it, out of sight of his cousin's searchlight gaze. There lay the loose pile of stones; from it crept the smell of the buried corpse, and a little dried blood as well, darkening the grass beneath it.

Patrick cast the stones aside and then, drawing his dagger from its sheath, began to pry the creature's hide from its bones. It was slow, clumsy work. The wolf had stiffened in its makeshift grave, and working the skin left his fingers covered in red nicks from where his blade slipped in its duties. But he didn't need the whole skin— just enough to pass for a leathery cloak, the price of a night-caught bride.

He wiped the dagger against the grass and stood, folding the hide in his arms. Over the wind, he heard Rowan's long, low *halloo*, calling a stray sheep from the edge of their grazing ground. Then he crept away again, knees aching, and returned to his bride.

Stella jolted to her feet when she saw him approaching. Patrick showed her the skin.

"Will it pass muster?" he asked.

She ran a curious hand through the fur and stayed quiet for a long moment.

"Nobody will think it's wings," she mused at last.

"But will it pass for a cloak?"

The harpy opened her mouth to reply—then her eyes went round, noticing at last the state of Patrick's hands. "What did you do to yourself?" she demanded.

"Stubborn skin." He hid his aching fingers under the flap of the hide. Stella glared, her upper lip twitching, her sharp yellow teeth peeking free.

"Is something the matter?" he asked nervously.

"Nothing," replied the harpy. "It's just..." She squeezed one wrist with the opposite hand, as if to stop it shaking. Her nose twitched like something tickled inside it.

"We should get to the village," she muttered. "So you can bandage yourself."

"All right." Patrick wedged the wolf-hide under one arm, wiping his hands fruitlessly on the knees of his hands. "Come up and walk with me then. You're my bride, after all."

Stella scowled at this, but she obeyed. She clung in his shadow as they stepped up the grassy rise, and soon they found themselves walking among the browsing ewes. They bundled close, nibbling his fingers and the hems of his cloak. None of them would approach Stella.

"They trust you," she murmured.

Patrick shrugged. "They'll trust you, too. They'll learn your scent."

Stella considered this. She wove a little closer, bumping Patrick with her shoulder.

"What's that about?" he asked.

All she would say was, "The wolf's skin. It's not quite right, but it'll do."

Then she could say no more. Rowan had turned toward them, shielding his eyes from the sun with one hand and raising the other above his head in greeting.

"Little cousin!"

With all the considerable grace of a house collapsing down a hillside, Rowan came bounding forward. The black raven's wing of his wool cloak smote the air; a few snowy lambs capered in his trail, bleating joyfully.

First came a constricting embrace that hoisted Patrick off his feet. Then, when his boots found the ground again, Rowan stood over them, grinning wickedly.

"You're late," he said with a thrust of his chin.

The lambs pranced nearby, nuzzling at Rowan's hands. One pushed its velvety muzzle into Patrick's palm, sniffing for a grape or a dandelion shoot. Laughing, he gently turned her aside. Stella clung close as well. Patrick felt her loop a bare slender arm through his, resting her chin on his shoulder. Her cloak's fur stood up sharp as fish spines, but on her face, she was every inch the new blushing bride, smiling easily at the two men.

An act, he knew—to fool Rowan, and whoever might come after. But it didn't stop the quivers shooting down his spine at her touch.

"Had to take it slow coming back," was all he replied. "Slippery going."

Rowan looked him head to foot. "Well...you're back in one piece, at least. I thought for sure we'd be scraping scraps of you off the rocks some morning."

Patrick shook his head. "No such luck for you. Rowan, this is Stella. My bride."

The words stumbled off his lips. But Rowan's grin only grew, mistaking his nerves for bashfulness. He cocked his head, his gaze rippling over every inch of Stella.

"A name?" he asked. "You're a strange one. But is she sweet like you hoped?"

Close to his ear, Patrick heard Stella's offended grunt. But her face kept its smiling mask, a rictus of placid, thoughtless beauty. She was the better actor of them by far.

"Even sweeter," he managed to stammer out. "Lucky me."

Rowan chuckled. "Lucky you—of course."

He clapped Patrick's shoulder with a paw big enough to drive fence posts. "Get into town straight away," he instructed. "The others will want their share of the good news, and there are preparations to make. And Old Matthew will want to meet her, of course…"

Before Patrick could reply, another hug engulfed him. This time, Rowan's bristling chin scraped his cheek, and his cousin whispered hoarsely in his ear.

"Her wings. Have you given any thought to where you'll hide them?"

Patrick hesitated, his heart kicking at double-rhythm. He shook his head guiltily.

"It's no matter," his cousin said. "Speak to your father—he knows all the best places."

He didn't let Patrick go, but held him out at arm's length, his hands on his little cousin's shoulders. He looked between him and his harpy bride, smiling fondly—but then a furrow twitched in his brow. His nose wrinkled, like he'd caught some stink, a note of rot in a flower bed. Rowan's eyes strayed to the wolf-skin folded under Patrick's arm.

Sweat slid down Patrick's neck, burying in his shirt collar. His nicked fingers stung.

Rowan asked hesitantly, "It's a happy match, then?"

"For a happy-after," Patrick responded automatically.

Stella's hands found his arm once more. She beamed so wide Patrick worried her face might split across the middle, like the lid on a jewelry box. But Rowan nodded slowly, his grin returning as well.

"I knew you'd do well," he said. "You're one of us now. I can see it plain on your face."

Then he turned to Stella. "And as for you..."

To Patrick's shock, he seized the harpy's chin in his hands, twisting her face upward like the hoof of a newly shod horse. Stella's eyes went wide, but she didn't jerk away—and though Patrick heard her breath catch, her smile didn't slip an inch. Rowan turned her this way and that, murmuring approvingly under his breath.

Then he pushed her aside just like she was another lamb.

"You're one of us, too," he said. "Welcome home."

Then he *halloo'd* to the flock, striding out among them like somebody wading into deep water. Patrick watched until the last ewe crested the next rise and slid from view. But his heart didn't slow, nor did the strange prickling jealousy in his belly smooth over—not even when the slate rooftops of Blackfrye began to appear through the trees.

Stella's smile stayed fixed in place. But the fingers gripping his arm bit just like teeth.

CHAPTER 10

"SEE HOW THEY WELCOME YOU!"

PATRICK'S VILLAGE had been small once—only a few dozen families nestled in the valley, beneath the splendor of the distant peaks. But that was long ago. Now Blackfrye sprawled, spreading like a shadow in the secret cleft of the mountains. Sturdy wood houses with foundations of hearty stone and cozy chimneys breathing endless gray smoke into the mountain sky. But as Patrick led his new bride down past the outskirts of the village, the brown streets were silent. Empty windows looked out from rough walls, reflecting only twilight.

At his shoulder, Stella whispered, "Where is everyone?"

"They'll be here," Patrick assured her. "The men come back from the fields at dusk."

"And the brides?" she asked.

As though in answer, a paleness flittered across one dark window. Moments later, that house's door crept open like a mouth ready to speak, only an inch or so, but enough to see a sliver of somebody's slender face peering out, framed by dark hair. Other doors cracked too, or shutters slid open on quarreling hinges. Curious faces peeped at Patrick and Stella from every direction as they wandered deeper. Nobody spoke. The only sound was the creaking of the tall trees and the distant complaint of a sheep.

Then, one by one, the wives of Blackfrye spilled into the street.

They appeared everywhere. It was like they had come down from the trees, or from holes in the ground. They were like the sheep with their dark eyes and white aprons, crowding and flocking like one mind commanded them all. But, as more and more tumbled from doorways and front porches, their silence seemed to grow and grow. They surrounded Stella, pawing at her with their hands, running amazed fingers across her fur cloak, their skirts and aprons whispering, their silent lips moving, always moving.

Stella whispered back. She was taller than all but a few of the younger wives; the rest had shrunk with age, stooping like their husbands. She ducked her head to meet them, to converse in that strange private huddle.

Patrick stood back in amazement. It seemed they might swarm over her like water flowing over a rock in a streambed. It seemed they might tear her limb from limb. Such fervor couldn't end any other way. Only a few times did one of the wives turn his way, but never more than a passing glance. One such was Rowan's tall, slender bride, with her one dark eye flashing out from behind the veil of her hair. Patrick watched Stella move among them, looking from face to face, catching hand after reaching hand in her grip. He caught glimpses of quivering lips, of cheeks stained and glistening, of wide, wanting eyes.

"I've come for Fay," his bride was saying to them. "Is she here? Where can I find her?"

Patrick's mother was not with them. And if the wives understood Stella's questions, they made no sign of it. They kept crowding nearer and nearer, tugging now at the cloak on her shoulders with clawing, desperate hands, and Stella kept asking, "Fay, Fay, has anybody seen Fay?" like it was a childhood game the others had forgotten the rules for.

"That's enough of that," boomed a distant voice.

The wives turned in one mass, flower-heads following the sun.

From the end of the narrow lane strode a scrum of men, holding lanterns upraised against the blossoming twilight. It was not every man in Blackfrye, but it was enough to darken the road with their bodies. At their head strode Old Matthew, his arms spread in welcome.

"Go on now." He flapped his hands, shooing the wives as though they were only stray geese blocking the path. "Go on—they're not here for you. Go on."

The wives dispersed like a whisper, scattering as quietly as they'd arrived. Most stole back into their houses, but a few joined the throng, finding their husbands and holding fast at their sides just like Stella had done. She clung to Patrick now. He felt her tremble slightly as the stomping crowd bore down on them. It seemed the correct thing—he found one hand and covered it with his own. Stella made no move to discourage him.

An act, he had to remind himself. It was an act, no matter how real it all seemed.

No matter how it made him feel.

Old Matthew strode a few paces ahead, bidding the crowd to tarry behind. A hard look graced his remaining eye. He lifted his lantern, letting the light play first across his son, then over his bride beside him. His breathing labored, almost a black bear's chuff as it left his lungs. He must have come from far away, doing some business elsewhere. He studied the pair for a long, pregnant moment. His bearded face hung so close to Stella's that Patrick thought their noses would touch. Stella's carved-on smile returned, utterly radiant set against the twilight.

But the hands on his arm shook like a newborn lamb's legs.

"She's wearing your ring," Old Matthew grunted. "Well handled."

Then he turned and faced the men of Blackfrye.

"My son's brought home a bride!" he roared.

The crowd seemed to explode, stomping and waving their lanterns. Shadows leapt and swayed against the surrounding tree trunks.

Old Matthew bade them be quiet with a wave of his hand.

"You old men of the village," he called out, "you remember this day in your own long-agos, what powerful feelings stirred beneath your ribs. Hold those feelings in your hearts for my Patrick now. And you others, you babes-in-arms! Take a lesson from my son's example. This is how Blackfrye grows. This is our strength—"

Old Matthew hadn't finished, but the crowd couldn't repress another eruption of noise. It was like a pot boiling with the lid on; something had to come up from beneath. Patrick's father turned toward him, grim pride branded on his face.

"The company of men," he intoned. "See how they welcome you!"

Then he raised his hands once more. And as though the old man were not a farmer but a mighty sorcerer, the crowd quieted, under his magic spell yet again.

"Well?" Old Matthew demanded. "What are you men waiting for? You there—fetch the laurels, and you—bring up some wine from my cellar, the oldest vintage, and you—some clothes for Patrick, that work shirt is soaked with sweat. And something too for the blushing bride! She's not going to wear some second-hand cloak on her wedding night, not if she's going to marry my son! Now, take them away! Get them ready, get them ready!"

Huffing like a pack of wolves, the grinning crowd shoved past Old Matthew and descended on Patrick and Stella. Many strong hands seized Patrick's shoulders, tousling his hair and thumping his back. Bearded lips breathed accolades and crude counsel into his burning ears. It was like the celebration in his father's home. The same noise, the same smells, the same pleasurable warmth building in his middle. And yet it was all more so. Stella was here beside him now. *His bride*—her hands clasped at his elbow, her hair brushing against his shoulder.

Again, Patrick found himself casting about for his mother. She should be here, he reasoned. Shouldn't she?

Not just to meet Stella—but to share this triumphant moment with him, to see how her gift and her cleverness had rewarded them all...

But Stella wasn't there anymore.

He realized a shade too late—the other Blackfrye men had torn her from his side. Others still held him fast in place. Patrick could only watch in muted horror and confusion as his bride was actually taken off her feet, borne away, thrashing amid a churning sea of bodies. Her eyes were wide and rolling; her long, yellow teeth snapped uselessly at her captors, but the men only laughed. Her face twisted this way and that, searching desperately *for him*, he realized with a molten stab of guilt. She was looking for him, and he wasn't there. One rough hairy hand stroked down her cheek, another grabbed her waist, and another and another again...

"*Let her be...*" Patrick said.

At first, his voice was only a whisper. The men holding his arms ignored him. He managed to wrestle free of their grasp, covering one guffawing whiskered face with his hand and pushing so hard the man tumbled head-over-rump to the ground. In any other moment, his strength might have surprised him. Instead, he only stood over his would-be captor, trying to unknot his fists, to quell the trembling that had set in all over his body.

The space around him cleared, and curious, angry eyes turned toward him. The man Patrick had pushed ran a hand under his nose, drawing it back stained red.

The shepherd put his shoulders back, standing as tall as he could.

"I said, let her be," he called above the men's murmuring. "You, and you—bring my bride back here to me. I'm not getting married tonight."

This froze them cold. The street became a painting, an elaborate still life as each dusky face twisted slowly toward him in turn. Two men crouched over a rolling cask of wine; another balanced an armful of laurels that he had to peer through to find his heading.

Old Matthew stood higher than the rest on a nearby porch, staring down at his son with no expression at all in his one visible eye. "Patrick," he began. "What's this about..."

Patrick's heart pounded, feeling like he'd shrink to nothing under so many stares. But he stretched his arm out toward Stella, and she wrenched free of her captors and ran to him, burying her face against his chest. Somehow, the rest came easier after that.

"It's been a long journey," he said. "I'm worn through—and my poor bride's in this new place, among so many new strange people... It simply wouldn't be right. Tomorrow. Tomorrow's a fine day for a wedding, but tonight we need rest."

He kicked dirt with the toe of one boot, his eyes cast down.

"And your patience," he added, "if you can spare it."

Old Matthew regarded him coldly. "Here's a very serious thing," he said.

But there was something beneath the hardness of his tone, a growl of recognition. It was the noise predators make in the forests or the fields, to know each other by.

Patrick gestured, mock-helplessly, to the harpy clinging to his chest. He shrugged—*what can you do?* His father's jaw thrust forward, his remaining eye a ragged slit in the dusk. But then he tipped back his head and roared with laughter.

"He asked for a sweet wife," he crowed. "See what comes of that!"

It seemed to satisfy the others. The men dispersed one at a time, chuckling under their breath and throwing pitying glances back over their shoulders. A few made fists near their eyes, *boo-hooing* in pantomime at him. Old Matthew watched from the porch as well, his judgment as silent and almighty as that of heaven itself.

Patrick didn't care. He only felt the weight of one set of eyes—Stella, his bride, tucked against his chest and looking up through her lashes and tears at him with a mixture of amazement and some other feeling he couldn't begin to name.

"Thank you," she breathed. Then she hid her face again.

Patrick only nodded in reply, his chin nudging into Stella's black hair. His arms enfolded the harpy, pulling her a little tighter to him. The other man's blood was drying on his palm.

A man does what he must.

They weren't Old Matthew's words now, or even his own. Now they belonged to some other thing living inside him, something that stretched and yawned as though it had just now woken up from a long sleep. And for the first time, Patrick thought they almost sounded true.

CHAPTER 11

ALONE TOGETHER

THE BEDDING HUT was the only circular building in Blackfrye. It was also the only structure in the village whose door locked from the outside only.

Old Matthew led them there. Stella no longer clung to her would-be groom, but hunched nervously after Patrick and his father, her bare feet picking along the dark and muddy street. Old Matthew took a key from his pocket and unlatched the sturdy door, which yawned open into a single round room: an ancient four-poster bed, a low table with an unlit lantern standing on it, and a metal pot lying kicked over against one curving wall.

"You'll sleep here tonight," he grunted. "Wouldn't be proper in the house, unwed."

Patrick nodded mutely. His father ushered them

inside, then handed the key over to his son, as well as a small soft bundle of clothes.

"For your bride," he said. Then he pulled Patrick's collar, drawing them nose to nose.

"Take heed of this. There's just one bed, but you're not a married man yet."

Patrick made no reply, feeling even in the dark his father's warning eye burning into him like a brand. Old Matthew huffed his good-nights, then stomped back out into the night.

Patrick and Stella were left alone.

The harpy collapsed on the bed, face up with her legs dangling—the bedframe wheezed and creaked, complaints built up from years of weddings past. Patrick shut the door and leaned against it in the oppressive darkness. He tried to think of anything to say.

"I've got clothes here," he said at last. "And shoes, if you'd like that."

Stella didn't answer. Instead, out of the dark came a sliding, stretching sound, like rawhide being stretched out to tan in the sunshine. Patrick thought to light the lantern, but by the time the flame hissed to life, Stella's shadow had changed. She loomed against the wall, crooked and batlike, her arms swallowed in the black sleeves of her wings.

Wearing this truer shape seemed to settle her a

little. She'd stopped quivering and now stalked back and forth in front of the lamplight, squared awkwardly on the knuckles of the curving claws that tipped each great lustrous wing.

"I've never been under a roof before," she said at last.

"How does it suit you?" Patrick asked.

Stella scowled venomously at the dark ceiling.

"I can't see the sky," she rumbled in her throat, and that was answer enough.

Then she fixed Patrick with a hard look. "Are all weddings like that?"

Patrick shrugged helplessly. "I don't know. I was too young to attend Rowan's."

"But you had some idea."

He couldn't look at her. The dagger, still dangling off his belt, seemed to drag him like an anchor. He fiddled with the buckle, but didn't take it off.

"I wasn't thinking," he admitted. "I'm sorry. I should have said something."

"One of us should have."

She laughed at her own remark—an ugly, unpleasant squeak, like somebody's porch door in a windstorm. "I guess it's easier to get through," she remarked, "if the bride can't talk."

Patrick frowned. "I like that you talk."

She kept up her pacing, crossing in front of the flickering lantern again and again, her hobbled gait made all the more uncanny by her monstrous black shadow that leapt and swooped across the concave walls. But her expression, which had been vicious before, seemed to have lost one or two of its sharper edges.

"Thank you," she muttered. "I...like that you talk, too."

She tromped to the bed again. She couldn't sit properly in that shape. Instead, she scrambled aboard the mattress in a funny kind of crouch, the weary springs groaning again in protest under her weight. Her wings bunched on either side of her, fanning out at the bottom like the hem of a dress, like a child's blanket dragged on the ground.

She said, "I guess I've made a lot of trouble for you."

"It's not so bad."

Long bat's ears flicked in the yellow lantern light. "If you say so."

Another silence followed. Not knowing what else he could do, Patrick joined her on the four-poster. Stella tucked her wings away to make room for him, and he eased down beside her, wary of the springs. One nervous hand stroked her wingtip by mistake—it was hairless and smooth and felt surprisingly brittle, like his finger could tear through the membrane without even trying. He snatched his hand away and tucked it in his lap.

"I'll get my mother for you now," he said. "If that's what you want."

To his surprise, Stella shook her head hard. Her fur prickled up, and she looked down at the floor, where the lantern's light danced in ripples like water.

"I don't know what I want," she said. "I just don't want to be alone right now."

So he stayed, looking straight ahead into the loping shadows on the hut walls, the little bundle of clothes still bunched in his lap. The lantern's flame licked the glass, and tree branches scraped the thatch roof and drummed the darkened windows.

Stella didn't speak again. But slowly, slowly, she tilted to the side, her wings folded tight around her, the weight of her hoary head coming down to rest on Patrick's shoulder.

Patrick didn't breathe. Before, such a gesture would've been only a ruse—to trick Old Matthew, or Rowan, or any of the other Blackfrye men, to make them see only the silent, happy bride she pretended to be. But now they were alone in this half-darkness.

There was nobody to pretend for any longer.

Had the hut grown somehow warmer? Did the

lantern's light flicker more beguilingly; had its shadow-children grown friendlier, more approachable, dancing slower and slower on the walls so even he could follow their clumsy, weightless steps?

Stella's wing shifted slightly beside him, leather membranes whispering, just in reach now of his fingers, slipping subtly beneath them—and her smooth cheek, sighing against his shoulder, was the softest thing he'd ever felt in his life.

Again it boiled up inside him, that nameless upwelling urge—to *take hold of her*, to fold her, wings and all, up into his arms, to draw her to him, into his lap, to tilt her lovely face towards his and press her lips against his own, or let them both fall backward into the warm soft embrace of the bed and, and, and—

The bed. This was the bed where Rowan had first taken his bride.

Where Old Matthew had taken his mother.

Something awful squirmed in Patrick. All those soft, pleasant pictures fled his mind, replaced now with terror, with shame—and a memory. It was harsh, laughing voices. It was heavy hands seizing his bride, tearing at her. It was her eyes searching wildly for him in the dark, her mouth hanging open in that soundless scream, a cry she could never give breath to, only so that their secret held, so that the game kept going, even to the very last...

And then into his mind came a second image. It was the faces of men, tilting up from that very creaking bed, with blazing eyes and beards drooping with sweat, their brides only a shadow beside them, their stares burning him across valleys of time. His grandfather, his cousin Rowan—Old Matthew, his ruined eye not patched but freshly scooped out, spilling dark and red from its horrible, empty socket.

Come take your turn, son, came the thundering command.

Come join in. Like us. Come take your turn.

Be a man.

Like us, like us, like us...

He stood with a jerk, so suddenly it verged on violence. It cost Stella her balance—she fell sideways on the bed, her wings jumbling. Patrick was already striding to the door, key in hand. He'd knocked his shins against the low table; the lantern coughed and quit, plunging the bedding hut into smothering dark again.

"What's the matter?" Stella called, rising from the bed.

He only paused for a moment. "My mother goes to bed early. I'll fetch her now."

"Wait," she protested. "Patrick, I..."

Maybe there was more to say. But Patrick was already gone. The door clicked at his back, and he left it unlocked, stumbling blindly into the darkness. The night was a hole he was standing at the bottom of. Sickness churned in the pit of him, threatening to boil over. He kept it down. He kept it all down, plunging headlong into the dark.

Once long ago, he'd seen a terrible wound—the gaping hole gored in a man's heaving flank by a ram's horn. Now he thought he knew exactly how it must have felt.

CHAPTER 12

PRIVATE ENGAGEMENTS

THE DARK LED HIM FORWARD, and forward and forward again. Houses rushed past him to his left and right. Windows flickered with life—in those dioramas, he beheld glimpses of warm little lives. Quiet dens, glowing golden in firelight, or lamplight, or the yellow breath of candles. Children played near comfortable hearths. Fathers smoked tobacco pipes or tossed their sons high in their arms. In each scene stood a wife, a mother—silent and still.

The images seemed to scoop him hollow. He didn't realize he'd reached his own home until his boots found the steps of the back porch. Here were the only dark windows in all of Blackfrye. He hardly saw the porch door opening until she'd flown through it, her arms cast out toward him in the gloom. His mother, wild-eyed, tangle-haired, clutching her white nightshirt closed and gesturing broadly with her other hand.

She pointed at her son, then out into the high distance, toward the grand shadow of the mountain and the nighttime beyond. *What kept you so long?*

For a moment, words wouldn't come. Then he simply swept forward into her arms. She caught him up, just like he was a child again, small enough for her lap or to hide behind her skirts. Her hair was damp after washing; it clung to his lips as he buried himself in her embrace. He still couldn't speak. He only held fast, lost in that comfortable dark, in the old familiarity of her love.

Then the bedding hut crept into his thoughts again, and he wrenched free, hiding his face.

"You've got to come with me, Mother," he said.

He tried to take her hand, to lead her out into the night. She wouldn't be led. Instead, she pulled away, standing back to observe her son, her hands clasped studiously. Then she put her wrists together, spreading her hands wide, a bouquet of fingers.

The flowers—was I right about the flowers?

Patrick nodded miserably. "You were right. She came. She's...she's wonderful."

Again, he reached for her hand. But his mother only

danced away, clapping her hands to her cheeks and grinning broadly at him. He'd never had reason to see it before, but her smile was Stella's—full of the same tiny teeth, yellowed and wickedly sharp. Before, it had only been a smile. Now he couldn't stand the sight of it.

There was movement beyond the dark glass of the nearby window. A creak, a footstep on a floorboard—the distant flicker of a lamp being lit. "Will you just follow me?" Patrick begged. "We shouldn't talk on the porch. It's not safe."

Look at you. A sharp, comical sigh; an exaggerated frown. *So unhappy.*

Patrick looked at his boots. "Why should I be unhappy? I'm going to be married."

A stiff finger poked his chest. Then his mother cupped her hands, like a child receiving a gift or placing a baby bird back in its nest.

And was she the wife you wanted?

"What do you know about what I want?" he demanded, twisting away from her. "What do you know about anything? I knew what I wanted before. I was going to have a bride, I was going to have a family. I was going to be a man. And then you came into my room with your flowers and your judgment, and you ruined it all. Now I..."

He pressed his palms to his eyes. Heat blazed under his collar. He tore at his shirt, popping the topmost buttons so that they bounced off the wooden boards at his feet. The night was a massive, sweltering hand, pressing down and down until it flattened him.

"Look what you've done to me," he moaned. "I'm coming apart."

He thought she'd protest, or spread her arms to him again. Instead, she watched him coldly, her dark eyes ragged in the greater surrounding darkness.

Finally, she nodded once, very slowly, with too much understanding.

I'm sorry. I'm sorry about it all.

Patrick scowled. He flexed his fingers, feeling all the little cuts stretch open again. The stinging sharpened him up, bringing the night back into focus.

"She didn't come here for me, Mother," he told her. "She doesn't love me. I've just made a bargain with her. She's here to speak with you."

His mother tilted her head. Her wet hair slid off her neck in one dark sheet.

She talks to you.

Patrick nodded. "Her name's Stella. She's told me your name, too."

Her eyes went perfectly round, and her lips dropped open.

Show me. She flung her arms out across the night-world, indicating the whole village with a single sweep of her hands, or all creation itself. *Show me. Show me.*

Patrick nodded again, numbly. "The bedding hut. That's where they—"

But she was already gone. Her white gown fluttered behind her, vanishing into the night.

He had to run to keep pace. He leapt off the porch, nearly losing his balance in the muddy yard. He'd never seen his mother so troubled or move so fast. Twice he almost lost her again as they wove through the dark streets together, but her white gown flashed against the night—a pale fish's belly, flickering on the water's surface.

Part of Patrick wondered what the other Blackfrye men would think—if they looked up from their own lives and out their windows, if they saw him chasing his own mother through the dark streets in her bedclothes. But this thought didn't tarry long. The sick feeling from before had returned, rotting inside him, black and nameless.

She arrived first at the hut. The door was still unlocked, but it was shut tight, and she waited at the entrance for him, shifting her weight from one bare muddy foot to its opposite. Leaves had gotten tangled in her hair. A grabbing branch or two had chewed up the hems of her nightgown. She didn't seem to care.

Please, she begged with her eyes. *Please, please, please...*

It hardly mattered, *please, what*. The want was enough, the enormous raw desire that seemed to suck her down into frenzy. She wet her lips, her hands flapping at her sides as though she still possessed wings, as if feeling alone could pull her into flight. Patrick strode forward, his own chest barrel-tight with anticipation. He took his mother's hand, and with the other, he unlatched the hut's door, pushing inside, into a second darkness.

Stella's hand struck the match that lit the lantern again. Light sprang up in their eyes. When sight returned, he saw her crouched over the low table, her wings folded in a high hump, the smoldering match still clutched in one stubby claw. Her jaw dropped open.

"*Fay...*" she breathed.

She didn't even glance Patrick's way. Instead, she flashed across the hut, wings spread like thunderclouds, tackling his mother to the ground. Patrick was nearly thrown aside in her haste. He stepped inside quickly as the two harpies embraced each other and shut the door behind him. Then he stood back and simply watched. Stella and his mother seemed to share one body—two pairs of legs, two pairs of joyful flashing eyes, all bound inside one pair of rippling black wings.

Then Stella's wings loosened their grip, and Patrick saw her face again—long ears fluttering, nose streaming green mucus, ugly and awful with tears.

"I'm sorry," she was crying out. "I didn't know, I didn't know."

Patrick's mother—*Fay,* he reminded himself, *she's called Fay*—smiled fondly at the harpy, and a little sadly as well. She eased them both to the floor of the hut, their conjoined shadow shrinking along the wall beside Patrick. Stella's head fell in his mother's lap, and she shut her eyes, letting Fay run fingers through her thick black hair.

Patrick's heart wrenched in recognition. How many times had he come crying to her, with a cut or some childish disappointment or anguish, and how many times had she comforted him in just this way? Slowly, the image before him began to change. He saw not only his mother but her double, her real winged self, hunched and black of hide, crooked and clumsy on land but sheer magic in the air. He saw her how she truly was.

Dark-creature, night-mother. Wonderful and terrible—and not like him at all.

Stella's sobs diminished. Fay's fingers stroked down her hairline, pulling raven locks away from his bride's long, leaf-like ear. She touched the red puckering scar, her lips pulling into a ghastly snarl. In the air, she closed her fist, twisting it like she would snap a branch in two, then brought it to her own breast.

This and her sad eyes said, *It's all right. He hurt me, too.*

Patrick took one shaking step back.

"No. No..."

It left his lips unbidden, so low that neither harpy could have heard him. But the thought, once conjured, couldn't be banished again. In Fay's lap, Stella's face turned slightly, enough to blearily stare up at him, through one half-closed eye, filmed with tears. Her lips moved, but no sound came out, and she turned away again and returned to her sobs. It turned his heart to wet clay inside his chest. In that moment, he accepted it.

He loved her.

He loved her, but she could never be his.

Wordlessly, he circled the outside of the hut, staying out of the lantern light. He found beneath the four-poster bed the discarded wolf-skin and lifted it into his arms. Then he returned to the doorway, casting one look back at Stella and Fay. Now his mother's face streamed tears too, silent sobs that could never have a voice.

She didn't look up. Neither did Stella.

So nobody saw him shut the door of the bedding

hut. Nobody saw him creep through Blackfrye's shadowed streets, barely a shadow himself, stooped like he dragged wings of his own from his aching shoulders. Nobody saw him steal up to his own front door, slipping in through it to his father's yawning greatroom.

So he did not vanish. It was instead like he'd never existed at all.

CHAPTER 13

MORE TRUTH

THE ROOM WAS NOT EMPTY. The fire bedding in the hearth was only glowing coals, but in their ghostly light, Patrick saw the hump of his father's sleeping form, reclined in his great armchair with his legs spread wide. His head had sunk to one side, and the thong of his lambskin patch hung loose. It slid down his cheek by a sliver, showing dusky red above it, and gaping blackness as well.

Patrick crossed the dim room on cat's paws. He laid a hand on his father's sleeping shoulder, who grunted awake—and seized his son's wrist in a steel grip.

"It's only me, Father," he cautioned, wincing.

Old Matthew didn't let go. His eye cast around the room, searching for phantoms in all the shadowed corners. "I thought she..." he panted. "I thought..."

Then his grip relaxed. His breathing slowed by

degrees, his shoulders loosened, and his eye, which had been smoky with sleep, grew gradually sharper. He reached up and returned the patch to its proper position, glaring up at his son with animal wariness.

"Why'd you wake me? You should be asleep as well."

Patrick swallowed. "It's not so late. I thought we could talk."

"Your mother's been restless at night these last weeks. I worried…"

Then his eye fell, spotting the wolf-skin under Patrick's arm.

"Where's your bride?" he demanded.

"Sleeping—and locked away soundly." Patrick patted his pocket, where the iron key still resided. "And Mother's asleep in her bed."

Old Matthew's suspicion softened, and he regarded his son fondly. "Well, that's well handled. Pull a chair over, then—you want to hear all the particulars of your wedding night, do you?"

Come take your turn, son…

Patrick gritted his teeth, but he nodded. He got a wicker chair and dragged it nearer to where his father sat. But before he settled into it, he took down an amber bottle off the mantlepiece, which had a film of dust around its bottom and a dustless circle beneath where it had stood. The glass caught the coal-glow, the right color for sunset.

"I thought," he said. "If we're talking like men, maybe we could drink like men."

Old Matthew grinned. "Well handled indeed. Give that here."

He got two glasses and returned to the hearth, measuring out generous pours for both Patrick and himself. They touched glasses and drank.

The whiskey was smooth and fine, like honey sliding down. His chest warmed, and Patrick's thoughts slipped back through time—to the night of his sixteenth birthday and his first taste of real drink. In that same darkened den, his father had shared what he knew about the ways of the world. About wives, about families, about Blackfrye and all the grand customs of manhood. How he had loved his father in that moment, how close they had grown, in the warm light of that special hidden knowledge. How astonishing the world had seemed, how full of prospect and wonder. Now, almost none of that old world remained.

Only the whiskey's taste was the same.

As he laid his cup aside, Patrick said, "It's not really the wedding night I want to talk about, Father. It's what comes after—all those days and nights after."

Old Matthew pursed his lips, disappointed. "Sure, we can talk about that."

He glanced again at the skin, now folded in his son's lap.

"You should have hidden that by now—and you, so close to your wedding."

Patrick nodded. "I wanted to ask about that, too."

Old Matthew took his time answering this. He swirled his whiskey, watching it dance against the rims of the glass, then drank the rest in one swallow.

"I know how you're thinking," he said. "It's better to hide those thoughts away. Doubt will keep you from doing what needs to be done. A man does what he must."

"I'm not doubting anything," Patrick said hastily. Then he got an idea. "I've been thinking about what we talked about before I left to climb the mountain. About how sheep only struggle once, how they come to love us once they realize what we're doing for them."

His father smiled, red-cheeked from drink, and scratched his beard. "It's good to hear you take my words so close to heart." He poured himself a little more and drank that too. "It's all true," he said. "But there's more truth beneath it."

"More?" Patrick leaned forward, his own whiskey forgotten.

Old Matthew nodded. "You learn it over the years. Every man has to learn it. There's the struggle at the start—you've seen that through already, up on the mountain. That's what the net's for, and the dagger too. But there's another campaign after. It's a long siege, against temptation. Even a sheep that loves her shepherd wanders off. And no matter how your bride loves you for what you give her: a roof, a bed at night, a family and children...no matter how special these things are to her, there's just so much open sky. Our duty as men, as their husbands, is to remove that temptation."

He drank, long and deep, of the sunset-colored whiskey.

"And they love us for that too," he said.

"Of course."

"That's why where you hide your bride's wings is so important. It's your wedding gift. You want it to be special, and you want it to last."

Patrick tried to smile but couldn't. All he could see was Stella's maimed and puckered ear, his mother's angry, silent eyes—*his grandmother, hobbling slowly toward a distant windswept cliff, a tablecloth around her naked, trembling shoulders...*

He put his lips to the glass but didn't drink.

"Let me ask, if I can—where would *you* hide them?"

Old Matthew pressed his lips in a line. It wasn't

really a smile—it was pride, maybe, or satisfaction, the look of a man remembering the finish of a fabulous meal. He reached down his shirtfront and pulled up a length of twine, from which a brass key dangled.

"In my wine cellar," he intimated in a hushed voice, behind his hand. "There's an old trunk your mother thinks is just full of old clothes. I thought you might lay your bride's wings there, next to hers. Wouldn't that be special?"

"Wouldn't that be special?" Patrick repeated.

"They're all like sisters, you know," his father went on. "They're different, of course—but alike in so many other ways." The whiskey had turned his eyes piggy, glazing them like windows in morning mist. "Laying them together. It might be special for them, too."

"Well—good night, then," Patrick said. He rose from his chair, turning to find the door as he set his own half-full glass aside. Then he paused, lifted it again, and sat once more.

"Father?" he asked.

His father lazed, his eye already half-closed. "Hmm?"

"Why are no women ever born here?"

Old Matthew's gaze sharpened once more, if only by a degree. "You're just full of questions tonight. If I knew that answer, I'd be the richest man in Blackfrye."

Patrick gazed right back. "But you are the richest man in Blackfrye."

His father chuckled softly. "Sheer stubbornness, then—does that answer it?"

Patrick shrugged. "Have another drink with me, Father."

He poured another finger into both glasses. The old man looked into his uncertainly, then at the bottle still in Patrick's hand. "I might save my real drinking for tomorrow."

"Please," said his son. "One more. With only me."

In mock-defeat, his father shrugged broad shoulders and took the glass up again.

"A man does what he must," he mumbled.

Soon he was snoring again, his empty glass nestled in his lap. The key on its twine rested against his round stomach. Patrick set both glasses aside so they wouldn't spill, then stood the bottle back up in its place on the mantle. Then he slid his dagger from its sheath and held it just next to Old Matthew's exposed neck—

—and with a twang, severed the twine holding the brass key in place.

He slipped it into his pocket with the other. His father didn't stir. The house was silent. His mother, Fay, was still in the bedding hut with Stella. Patrick kicked the coals in the hearth, cooling them black. Then, like a ghost, he was gone.

CHAPTER 14

PATRICK'S TURN

HE WISHED he'd brought a lantern.

The cellar wasn't connected to the house—it was dug some yards away, easy enough to spot in the daylight, but under cover of darkness it was nearly invisible, laid flat to the earth, just enough patch of level ground in the middle of the village. Patrick rarely descended into that fusty cavern, so he had no practice finding it, in light or in shadow. When he located it at last, it was by kicking the shut door by mistake, hard enough to bruise his toe right through his boots.

He sucked his teeth and swore so loud that one or two windows lit up, and curious shadows moved behind them. But nobody came out to see what the fuss was.

The double doors to the cellar lay unlocked; still, they were heavy enough that he had to strain to open even one. Behind them, earthen steps led down a hollow throat into the ground. This wasn't night-darkness—it was dark like the black behind his own eyelids. He hefted the wolf-skin, then traced the heartiest blessing he knew across his chest.

Then he started down.

Recent rain had softened the ground. His boots sank with every step. But at last he'd descended fully, and the cellar gaped ahead of him. By chance, he bumped another lantern hanging near the entrance, and it coughed up dusky light when lit, exposing the cramped maze of wood shelves that lay before him. Some of the wine was in bottles; some was in great round-bellied casks. A wall at the back had partially collapsed, spilling earth into the room. Those shelves were in disarray, crooked as an old man's teeth. The lantern's flame danced crazily, making shadows leap out at him every time he swung the light to look somewhere else.

Shadows with fangs—shadows with bats' wings.

He shivered and soldiered on.

Of course, the trunk would be in the back. Old Matthew was far too cautious for him to find it anywhere else. But as Patrick waded further into the dark, he prayed he wouldn't see it at all—he prayed it would be empty, or only contain the spare clothes his father had deceptively told his mother were there. Then it could be true that there had been some mistake, that the world was actually far kinder and softer and gentler than he knew it was now.

But every shadow was a wolf's jaws now. Or worse— one of his cousins, twisted into a monstrous shape by the cellar dark, with pawing hands and leering eyes and a gaping, drooling mouth. All around him hung silence like mist after rain. Even his footsteps made no sound.

It made his thoughts echo all the louder, as well as the fearful drumming of his heart.

Then, at last, it appeared in the far corner, covered by a draped canvas tarp. The trunk was smaller than he'd thought. He'd imagined something large enough to conceal a whole person; this was hardly the size of a cradle. But it looked sturdy, leather-bound, with thong handles on either side of its lid, not some cheap pine box that could be kicked apart with a boot, and the lock joining its lips glinted in the lantern-light.

He knelt before it, laying aside the wolf-skin and the light and fishing the key up from his pocket. He could feel his heartbeat everywhere—in his throat, in his skull, in the fingers trembling around the key. It took two tries to slot it, and quite a bit of effort to unlatch the rusty mechanism. But at last a click echoed, and the lid sprang open like a trap.

It was clothes inside after all: the top layer gave up old white shirts, rumpled brown pants, and tight, bunched balls of white wool socks. Next came items Patrick recognized, clothing he'd worn as a small boy and outgrown. Trousers torn at the knee, old boots still muddy from playing in the fields, shirts with clever patches on the elbows, sewn by his mother in candle-light evenings. But when these were laid aside, his next discovery stopped him cold. He lifted it out gingerly, as though it would crumble at his touch.

A long white dress, rustling with lace, with puffed shoulders like bloodless roses in full lascivious bloom. The bottom hem was crusted with brown dirt—dirt, and something else.

His gorge rose, and he hurled the dress aside with a wordless cry. When he kept digging, it was with nervous hands. Closer and closer now to the floor of the trunk, until—yes. His fingers brushed against soft fur instead of corduroy or coarse linen. Fur that stood straight when he touched it, fur that bristled and twitched against his hand. Hurriedly, he dragged it free, tossing garters and long stockings to the side in his great haste.

Then he held it in his hands. It wasn't black like Stella's was—this cloak was silver, like moonlight, and textured like a cat's coat, matted in a few places and squashed-down in others, but soft under that, and sleek, and so very beautiful. Overcome, he pressed it to his cheek.

It even smelled like her, like his mother. Like Fay.

The cloak fluttered against him, like it had caught some unfelt breeze. It twitched in his grip—it shifted, it stretched. Then it wasn't a fur cloak anymore at all. It was the silvery wings of a huge and magnificent bat, flapping weakly in his grasp. It made his fingertips tingle and buzz, just touching and holding it in his hands. He could almost imagine the rush—to slide inside them, his arms melting away like a caterpillar inside its cocoon, and then *changing*, unfurling in ecstasy like a flower until—

Soft footfalls pulled him out of the reverie. The light touch of a slender hand ghosted against his shoulder. He whirled, his heart clenched tight in his teeth.

"What are you doing here?" Stella whispered.

She loomed above him, bent over beneath her own cloak beside his flickering lantern, its frantic light sending the shadows lurching across her features. Her face was still dirty with tears, gleaming like mica. But now her expression was inscrutable.

"You didn't come back," she went on. "And I thought—I mean, we thought…"

Then she looked down, into his lap. The wings seemed to doze, calmed by Stella's voice, still and silent as a newborn lamb curled against its mother's belly.

Stella's red lips opened in a dark letter O. "Those aren't..."

Patrick nodded silently. Stella gaped—she knelt at his side, reaching out one bold hand to stroke her fingers along the ridge of one flexing membrane. The wing shuddered as she made contact, all the nearby hairs rising as though to greet her.

Her head whipped up to meet his gaze—her stare carved into him, sharp as teeth.

"I don't understand," she whispered.

Patrick shrugged limply. "I don't understand either."

"It's a trick," she sputtered. "That's all. It has to be..."

But as her eyes darted between his face and the wings draped across his knees, all her protests died in her throat. "Why are you doing this?" she demanded. "Why?"

There were a hundred reasons. None of them had names. Instead, he looked down, watching his mother's wings fuss in his lap. Their tips beat against the floor like a moth on its back, like they might launch up into the air at any moment if set right. He clutched them to his chest, but they only flapped all the harder, bruising his sternum and ribs.

"She's my mother," he said at last. "I...I have to."

"You'll lose her," Stella said.

But Patrick only shook his head. "No. No. I lost my grandmother."

For a moment, Stella only stared. In the lantern's whipping light, her expression changed with every lashing shadow that crossed it. Then she leaned out across the dark toward him. Her eyes burned—with something like hatred at first, then sorrow, then confusion, and then some other feeling he couldn't describe. Suddenly, she seized him roughly by the shoulders, her fingers biting sharply into his skin. But now new tears stood at the corners of her eyes, glistening, threatening to spill.

"Do you remember what you asked before?" Her voice shook with fury. But it was only a shell. Something thin and delicate, protecting something even *more* delicate beneath. "About why I came back to the mountaintop?"

Patrick nodded. He scarcely dared move. Her face floated closer, bathing him now in the very warmth of her breath. "I didn't know the answer then," she was saying. "But I think..."

He held his breath. Stella's red lips were inches from his own.

"I think I was looking for somebody just like you..."

Then she froze. In an instant, whatever magic occupied that dark, cramped moment dissolved back into nothing. Stella turned back toward the darkness that crowded just beyond the cozy circle of the lantern. Patrick looked too. Had that been a cough on the stairs?

Was that the flicker of a second lantern?

Was that Old Matthew's footstep in the cellar entranceway?

"Patrick...?" he called, his voice ragged with sleep. "Patrick, are you there?"

CHAPTER 15

BRIDES IN THE DARK

AT THE SOUND of Old Matthew's voice, Fay's wings took up in a frenzy. They flapped and fluttered and tore at the air with such ferocity Patrick thought they'd whirl up toward the earthen ceiling. He got his whole arms around them to stifle the noise, and they butted under his chin, slapping against his ribs so hard he thought they'd break. But he didn't cry out.

His father stepped off the stairs into the cellar room with weary, rolling steps. His talk was slurred; he seemed to keep his head straight only with great effort. Another lantern swung from his fist. The other hand scraped across his round stomach.

"I gave it a little consideration," he was saying. "Maybe we'd better not keep two pairs of wings so close together. I can tell you some fine spots I've dreamed up, and..."

His gaze snapped in Patrick's direction. Without thinking, Patrick pulled Stella down out of sight and doused his own lantern, plunging them into darkness.

His father chuckled in his throat. "Now what's this about? I saw your light only a moment ago. Come out and stop playing games—what's the matter with you?"

The whiskey seemed to have married his mood. He'd set the lantern down on the cellar floor at his feet, and now he stalked slowly forward, whistling tunelessly, creeping on exaggerated tiptoe, with his hands crooked into claws in front of him.

"You want to play hide and seek? All right—I'm going to count to ten."

Fay's wings struggled in his arms. Stella grabbed hold too, but even with her added strength, he couldn't keep them still. She stared at him wide-eyed—her gleaming eyes were all he could see of her in the dark. He tried to think. Thoughts wouldn't come. He could only hold on tight, his lungs aching harder and harder, not even daring to breathe.

Old Matthew crept closer and closer again. The lantern threw his enormous shadow across the room, a stalking predator—another two-legged wolf, rippling across the walls.

"Here I come, Patrick," his father giggled. "Here I come, ready-or-not..."

Stella's hand found Patrick's. Her expression changed in the dark—resolute now, instead of fearful. She threaded their fingers together, then pulled free and clambered to her feet.

Before he could stop her, she'd stepped out from behind the shelf of wine casks and walked straight into the heaving yellow circle of Old Matthew's lantern.

His father paused. He looked her up and down, like she was some unusual beast who'd wandered into his garden. "Hel-lo," he began. "Now, how'd you get down here?"

Stella cocked her head and beamed. But she didn't speak.

Old Matthew rocked back on his heels. With the lantern at his back, Patrick couldn't see his smile—but he could imagine it from his voice. "You're not supposed to be wandering around, you know," he cooed. "Your future husband ought to be more careful with you."

He reached out for her—she smiled teasingly, side-stepping just in time, just enough that she began to lead Old Matthew away from the light, away from the stairs that led up and out of that dark tomb. As she did this, she locked eyes with Patrick, still crouched in his dark corner.

Below her cloak, one hand crooked to him. She

couldn't sign like Fay, but there could be no mistaking what she wanted.

Get out. Get out. Get out.

Old Matthew lunged for her again, chuckling at the sport. Stella's eyes rounded, but she dodged him again, keeping her smile bright and her eyes laughing.

"You liked my boy's gift, did you?" The old man rubbed his hands together. "You liked the look of him. I wonder, how do you like the look of me?"

Patrick tightened his grip on Fay's wings. He willed them still—*just a little longer, please, just a moment longer*. He rose from his crouch and hobbled forward, terrified he'd kick a shelf or a loose bottle on the floor and give up the whole game. Stella ducked another grab from Old Matthew, and another and another. Each step took her deeper into the dark; each miss took his father farther from the cellar's exit.

"We're going to be family, you know," Old Matthew was saying, starting to pant from effort and the excitement of the hunt. "You ought to go easier on me, I'm an old man…"

Then—the unthinkable. Stella ducked under arms that meant to bearhug her. She stepped back and stumbled over a crate that had tipped off one low shelf. She lost her balance, wobbling frantically on one bare heel.

Old Matthew surged forward with a roar of triumph—

"Got you," he crowed. "You teasing little thing."

He seized her in smothering arms, hardly noticing how she whimpered in sudden terror at his touch. One hand wrapped around her slender wrist. The other gripped her chin, like Rowan before him. Her head jerked back, trying to wrench free, her dark shining hair sliding off her shoulders, falling away—

"Now," Old Matthew purred. "Let's see if you're as sweet as..."

—*from her scarred ear*. Patrick's breath caught like a hook in a fish's jaw.

His father stood perfectly still. His voice was like stone.

"You. I might have known."

Stella's eyes rolled in panic. She thrashed, she kicked—butting and biting, just like a lamb who'd never been shorn. But even in his advancing years, Old Matthew's grip was still beyond compare in Blackfrye. Her struggles meant nothing. He hardly noticed at all.

"You thought you'd fool me," he was saying. "You thought you could just walk in under my nose—marry my only son right in front of me. *My son!*"

Patrick was ten feet from the cellar stairs. He could see light filtering down from the top, from the moon's beckoning gaze. But Old Matthew was shaking Stella now, so that her head whipped back and forth like a cloth doll's, her eyes glazing, her jaw going slack, all that fight and fury battered out of her, helpless against his strength.

"I'm sorry about this, Patrick," he called out—to the darkness, to no one.

His mouth set in a grim line. His hands slid toward Stella's throat.

"We'll lure you a better bride," he vowed. "I'll see to it myself."

"Patrick..." Stella gasped. "Patrick, help me, please..."

Old Matthew paused. He dragged Stella closer, inspecting her like an insect skewered on the end of a pin. "So—he let you keep your wings," he seethed. "That son of mine. He was always too much like his mother. *But it's just one more mistake to correct...*"

"*Pah...*" she begged.

Then she could beg no more. With a grunt of effort, Old Matthew tightened his grip on the harpy's throat. Her struggles stopped, her eyes rolled back white as ice, and her red lips trembled, yawning in a silent, endless gasp. Old Matthew started to smile again.

He didn't hear his son coming up behind until Patrick's arms wrapped around his neck.

A confusion of limbs, a writhing hydra of bodies. Old Matthew spun lazily, purple-faced and gagging—his son's weight twirled him into the embrace of the hard-packed cellar wall. Their heads knocked against it. Dirt rattled down from the ceiling. Patrick's hands slipped, and he rolled off his father's back, landing in a dazed heap.

Stella wormed free, wriggling away on her back. Old Matthew was still between her and the door. She fell against a shelf of bottles, gasping, her hand cupping her crushed throat.

Old Matthew staggered. He braced against the wall, then spat a line of clear mucus onto the cellar floor. His boots ground the dirt as he turned toward Patrick slowly.

His lambskin patch had torn away—it dangled loose from one bruised ear, the inside of it flaking brick-red with rot and long-dried blood. Beyond it yawned a horror. Flaking skin, and pulp and jelly, over which the lip of the useless eyelid sagged loose like the flap of a tent. A thick-knuckled hand plucked the patch and flung it away, pulling the skin with it, stretching it, tearing it away with a sound like ripping burlap.

"What in the world..." he murmured, mostly to himself.

On the ground lay Fay's silver wings, jerking weakly

in the dust. Old Matthew took one woozy step toward them. Patrick staggered to his feet, blocking his father's way.

The old man grunted—in sheer disbelief, hardly even angry at all. His single eye roved, the ruin of the other staying fixed in place, staring past Patrick's shoulder.

"What are you doing with those?" he murmured.

"Father, let us pass."

Old Matthew gawked. He rubbed his temple and shook clods of dirt out of his hair. "What is this?" he demanded. "What could you possibly think you're doing?"

Patrick didn't answer. He looked past his father, at Stella lying in the dirt.

"Are you all right?" he called to her. Stella only coughed in response.

Old Matthew's stupefied stare swung back towards the wounded harpy on the floor, then returned to his son, the expression on his dark, bearded face hardening.

"Well—we've learned some lesson tonight," he said. "I warned you, didn't I? They can trick you with their words. They're clever when they want to be—in some ways, they're even more clever than a man. So tell me. What kind of bargain did she make for this foolishness? That she'd make you happy? That she'd be a good wife to you, *a sweet wife*, if only this, and this, and this? Did she promise to *love* you?"

He took a step forward. Patrick held his ground, his hands fumbling along his belt. Only when his fingers touched the hilt of the dagger did Old Matthew stop his advance. "Haven't you been listening?" the old man said. "They *can't* love you. Not until we show them how."

The dagger slid from its sheath with a whisper. Patrick stared at it, seeing only his eyes reflected in the dull metal of the blade. If he covered one, they could be his father's eyes staring up at him. But they were not. They were different enough after all.

There were a hundred things he wanted to say then, a thousand manly boasts. But words seemed so far away now, and boasting so small. So instead, he tightened his grip on the hilt of the dagger. He pointed the tip of the blade at the old man's neck.

"She was never going to love me anyway," he said.

Old Matthew's lip quirked up in a dangerous half-smile.

"Then, that's it. You think you'll take my wife from me—just like that?"

Strange calm washed through Patrick. He pulled up to his full height and looked his father in the eye—not his living eye now, but the dead one. The one Stella had taken from him.

"I'll do what I must," he replied.

His father's shoulders slumped. His head drooped, a parody of a defeated soldier. Then his beard shook with a laugh like a sword being drawn from its sheath.

"Your mother ruined you after all," he said.

Then he lunged like lightning.

The dagger flashed through the air. It sank home—in Old Matthew's bulky shoulder, sliding in straight to the hilt with a sickening wet slice. Patrick's father set loose a howl of pain, but when he jerked back, the weapon pulled free, fell from Patrick's grip, and spun across the floor, out of the circle of the lantern-light. Then the old man was upon him.

Hands like slabs of mutton seized Patrick's skull and shoved him back into the shelf of wine bottles behind him. White light burst across the back of his skull as he bounced off the sharp wood of the topmost shelf, sliding awkwardly past each rung until he'd collapsed against the bottom. Before he could move, a kick exploded against his ribs. The shelf above him tilted crazily; wine bottles tumbled down, blasting open against the floor on his left and right. Cool red wine rained over him like blood. Warm, warm and wet—maybe it was blood after all.

He couldn't tell if it was his father's or his own.

Another kick caught him, this time under the chin. He crashed back limp, his head lolling, his eyes battered closed, looking at the world through narrow slits. The lantern's light danced viciously across the walls. He saw his father only as a hazy towering shape, a shadow cast on the walls of his perception. Patrick tried to look for Stella, hoping he'd see her flitting past—up the stairs, taking to wing, to safety. But Old Matthew was all there was to see.

"You're not a man," said a voice from inside the shadow. "And you're no son of mine."

He loomed closer, filling Patrick's fading vision. Then he stopped. His mouth jerked open, but nothing came out—nothing but a clear trickle of blood and spit. From the center of his neck, something began to bulge outward. It was the point of Patrick's dagger, pushing through the skin until it burst clear on the other side like a young shoot bursting through the soil. Blood spurted in a thin, hot line across Patrick's face. Old Matthew gagged, his good eye mushrooming out of its socket.

Behind him, huge silver wings stretched wide, eclipsing all light.

The shadows crushed in fast around him, and Patrick's eyes drifted closed. But even in that new darkness, he thought he saw Old Matthew slump sideways, each wet breath rattling in drowning lungs. He thought he saw a terrible shape—a shape wearing a bat's magnificent wings, awful and radiant all at once—crowd forward, hunching down over the wounded old man, pressing red, ravenous lips against his spurting neck. And he thought he heard a voice speak words that frightened and thrilled him all at once.

It was a voice he'd never heard before. He'd been hearing it all his life.

"*Hello, darling,*" said his mother.

Then dark rose up like a storm of leathery wings, and Patrick knew no more.

My husband...

A child is the most precious gift a bride can bestow upon her husband. I took a piece of you, and I let it grow inside me until it was half of what you are and half of what I could make him. He was mine because I invented him, because he hatched from my aching loins, from my love alone. But he was also yours, because I was yours, because by some unknowable power, everything your gaze fell across became your own in one shape or another.

In this way, I've repaid whatever small kindness you've seen fit to show me, whatever love you thought you held for me. That debt was paid in full.

And now, I have reimbursed all the rest as well.

CHAPTER 16

MIDNIGHT

IT WAS three days in the shivering dark—three days, and three desolate nights. Patrick's whole world had shrunk down to a circle six feet across. One end of a chain fixed to the iron cuff on his wrist; the other was shackled to the far leg of the four-poster in the bedding hut. The door was locked from without, and somebody had nailed boards over all the windows so no light could get in. Twice every day, the door would swing open—a bath of terrible light would wash inside, and somebody would shove over a tray of cold food. Other than that, he was left alone.

Sometime in that first morning, two Blackfrye men had come down into the cellar and discovered him, covered in wine and blood in equal part. They had dragged him to the surface and asked him a lot of questions he didn't know the answers to. And when they couldn't jostle a satisfactory reply out of him, they bandaged up his wounds and locked him away inside endless night.

He hadn't spoken to a soul since.

Toward the end of the second day (or night, there was almost no way to be sure) his eyes started to play tricks on him in the grueling dark. Sometimes he swore he saw the muscular curve of a bat's wing projected on the wall, or the flash of tiny sharp teeth, slick with saliva, or heard a soft voice echoing off the hut's curving walls. Once, waking from a nightmare, he'd cried out Stella's name—the only answer he got was mocking laughter from some man outside his cell, standing guard.

Patrick didn't mind it. It was good that Stella was gone—and his mother.

His mother. His mother, who had found her wings.

His mother, who had stabbed his father through the throat, and drank hot lifeblood from his body as it twitched on the floor under the earth...

If he hadn't been in that cellar, he could've thought it was just another dream. But every time his eyes shut, Patrick saw the night unfurl like blood-red thread off a spool. There was his mother, his true mother—crouched over his father's slack body with her massive silver pinions covering Old Matthew almost completely and her red lips pushing hard against the wound in the big man's spurting neck. A wet grunt as her jaws widened the cut, followed by a thick sucking sound that bubbled and spat like stew over a hot fire. His mother's body convulsed once, twice, drawing whatever was inside her husband inside herself instead.

His skin went taut, then almost colorless. His eyes pulled back inside their sockets.

He groaned once, a hollow rattling sound, trying to limply crawl away.

"Look away, darling," Fay said, between swallows. "Look away, please..."

But Patrick did not look away. Not even when his mother picked up her head, heavy and dripping with blood and torn flesh, and turned to a darker corner of the cellar.

"You next, little one," she whispered kindly.

And slowly, Stella crept forward on her wingtips and began to drink as well.

She's still beautiful. It was the last thought Patrick had before the lantern went out and the memory went full-dark again. *Somehow they're both still so beautiful.*

Then came the third night. Patrick had just gobbled the last crumbs of the second meal of the day—smaller this time than all the others, barely a crust of stale bread and a mouthful of dried mutton. They had decided his fate, he imagined. Tomorrow, there would be no more need to feed him.

But just as he'd swallowed the last mouthful of water from the jug they'd provided, a key rattled in the lock, and the door moaned on its crusty hinges. A shape entered, dragging a wicker chair behind him. He shut the door and set his seat opposite Patrick, sitting with his arms crossed and his chin thrust forward. It wasn't until he spoke that Patrick realized who it was.

"They're still looking for Old Matthew," Rowan said.

Patrick nodded slowly. Even though his eyes had adjusted to the dark, he couldn't read his cousin's expression at all. The hood of his cloak swallowed his face in shapeless shadow, showing only his whiskery chin beneath.

"I don't think they'll find him," he replied, his voice creaking from disuse.

Rowan looked away. "No—I don't expect that they will."

A long silence followed. Then Rowan reached under the shelf of his cloak, pulling out a small metal flask that he pushed toward Patrick. "You could use a drink, I imagine."

When Patrick eyed it warily, Rowan said, "It's not poison. They don't want you dead."

Puzzled, Patrick drank. It was the same whiskey from his father's mantle. He almost spit it back out, but managed to swallow it down. The warmth did him good. It uncurled his limbs on the bed, letting him sit up straight.

"Why'd you do it?" Rowan asked softly.

"I didn't kill Old Matthew."

"That wasn't your dagger they found in the wine cellar?"

"You know I didn't. I couldn't."

"You know what I mean," Rowan said levelly.

Patrick drank from the flask again, then capped it in his lap.

"I loved her, Rowan," he answered.

"That's what you told the others. I'm your cousin—give me a real answer."

"I don't have any other answer."

Rowan let his breath out in a huff. "All men love their wives. That's nothing special."

Patrick considered this for a long moment.

"I think..." he said at last. "I think maybe I made her love me."

His cousin rocked back in his seat. "What's that like?" he asked.

"It's like having your legs broken."

Rowan stood up with a jerk, knocking the chair

away. In a sudden fury, he seized hold of Patrick's collar, dragging him up off the bed by almost a foot.

"Be serious!" he demanded. "They might still kill you. It all depends on you cooperating tomorrow. Don't give nonsense answers like that, or who knows what might happen."

"I am being serious," Patrick answered, once Rowan had let him down again. "It's...it's a helpless feeling. Like you can't hold your own weight anymore. But you don't mind it—because there's somebody else there, bearing you up, making you strong. You let go, you let yourself fall, and suddenly you're stronger than you've ever been in your whole life. And it doesn't hurt at all. Well, it hurts a little. But you'd rather feel that than nothing, because it comes from her, and not from inside yourself. It feels—"

"Have another drink," his cousin muttered. "You're babbling."

"It feels wonderful," Patrick insisted, sitting forward. "Can't you understand? The world gets so heavy. Maybe we're not supposed to carry it alone."

Rowan didn't speak. He only put his hand out for the whiskey.

Patrick handed it over, and his cousin drank.

"It doesn't sound so bad," he said in a low voice. "The way you tell it."

Patrick nodded slowly. Rowan watched him for a long moment, over the top of the flask.

"Do you know what they want to do with you?" he asked. "It's all decided. They want to send you up the mountain again—with a couple of other men, to make sure you do the job. It'll be like with your grandfather. They'll send me, and two others. They mean for you to lure down another bride. You can still sire children. You can still make Blackfrye strong."

"I can still be one of you." Patrick rolled over on the bed, away from his cousin, facing the opposite wall. Rowan groaned and slumped noisily in his chair.

"But you won't do it," he grouched. "You'd rather sulk here, wasting away—or get stoned to death, or pulled apart by horses, or whatever else they think up to kill you off. You mind telling me why?"

Patrick shifted on the bed. "You'd never believe it."

"No," Rowan agreed. "I guess I probably wouldn't."

Patrick heard whiskey sloshing at the bottom of the flask.

"This was supposed to be for your wedding day. Now it's almost gone." Rowan's voice was thick with drink now. "Well—it was good while it lasted."

His cousin rose unsteadily from his chair and stood over Patrick a long moment without talking, and when he finally broke his silence, it seemed to be only to himself.

"What am I going to do with you?" he muttered.

Then something hard crashed down against the back of Patrick's skull.

When awareness returned, the world had spread out again. The too-close dark of the bedding hut was gone, replaced by endless rolling gray. Patrick tried to sit up, but pain rang a terrible note in his aching skull, and he had to lie down flat again. It wasn't a bed beneath him but curving wood, and every time he moved, the world seemed to rock and keel with sickening rhythm. He heard wind and nearby water but nothing else.

Finally, he managed to pry his eyes open and see where he was. The endless gray expanse was the cloudy sky and the cloudy sea below. At his back loomed craggy black cliffs, a towering shelf of shadow against the lighter sky. He was drifting out with the tide. From the gunwales hung wooden oars. At his feet lay a small wicker basket that sounded full when he prodded it with his toe.

And beside this—the still-bloody skin of a huge black wolf.

He looked back at the cliffs, catching a flash of tiny movement at their peak. Two slender shapes observed him from the edge, dark like the cliffs themselves were dark, rendered featureless in the twilight, against all that gray sky. He couldn't see their faces. But Patrick saw his cousin lift his hand over his head and wave it slowly back and forth, then trace a sign in the air. A blessing, for good fortune. A farewell.

And perhaps it was the twilight gloom—but Patrick thought he saw Rowan's wife tuck a cloak tight around her slender shoulders, lean toward her husband, and put her face near his, as though to whisper something in his ear. But they were so far up, and so far off. Patrick couldn't know what he'd seen or not seen. Maybe Rowan was alone.

He watched as the pair waved to him once more.

Then they turned back toward Blackfrye, hand in hand, and vanished.

CHAPTER 17

STRANGE SIGHTINGS

THERE WAS food enough in the basket for three days.

Then it was all gone.

Patrick had rowed through the first two days, and slept through the first two nights under the shelter of stars and the stiffening wolf-skin. But once the food was all eaten, he let himself drift. He didn't know where he was really sailing to, anyhow. He could navigate to Wicke by the stars, but Wicke men hunted their wives in the forests. And Burning Coast fishmongers took theirs from the sea. He wondered what a forest bride might look like, or a sea bride. He wondered what it was they gave up for their husbands.

He scanned the flashing water, but no lovely faces swam up beneath the hull of the rowboat. All he saw was a few schools of fish and little white-capped waves.

His stomach complained, but it wasn't hunger that

was picking him apart. It was his thirst. In the bedding hut, the dark had plagued him, tormenting him with visions. Now his foe was the endless horizon. During daylight, the sun baked down—the drier his throat became, the more often he began to glimpse horrible shapes emerging from the waves only a dozen yards away from the stern, bobbing up as part of some inexorable pursuit. Or he would feel some heavy muscular body bump against his craft in the night, hard enough to shudder him awake. Sleep came fitfully after that, and the hungry aquatic horrors behind his eyelids were no friendlier company than his waking dreams.

Soon, he couldn't stand it any longer. One morning, without even realizing what he was doing, he leaned over the side of the rowboat and scooped huge mouthfuls of seawater down his throat. But this relief didn't even last the hour. His guts twisted and rebelled inside him, and he vomited a thin, clear stream of salty misery over the side, where it foamed against the hull of the boat and stank for hours after.

It was the first time he allowed himself to weep. He wasn't used to doing so, especially out in the open. But on the wide flat wate,r there was nobody to hear him. It happened suddenly. One moment, he was balefully watching the horizon rising and falling with the bobbing of the boat. The,n with no warning at all, he was thinking of her.

Stella—dropping out of the sky on the high midnight peak.

Stella—covered in mountain dirt, seething at him on the black slopes.

Stella's arm looped through his, her smile straining in front of the men.

Stella's face, streaked with tears, peering up at him from the comfort of his mother's lap.

The graceful curve of her velvet wing, the lustrous drape of her dark, tangled hair, the sharp mockery of her ink-stain eyes.

The temptation of her red lips, leaning toward him in the cellar dark...

He gripped the splintery rail and sobbed. His throat was too dry to make much sound, but it bent him double, that sudden terrible emptiness. He'd never see her again. It scraped him hollow; it ate him up from the inside out like a plague, like a burning fever. The corners of his eyes stung, pinched, and cracked with no tears to shed. He didn't even have to dry his face after.

Then his dreams only grew stranger.

Evening came—the fourth, or maybe the fifth. There was no way of knowing, out on the featureless ocean. He lay in the damp bottom of the little craft, halfway between waking and dozing, his tongue cleaving in his jaw and every inch of skin itching and red from the sun. Without warning, some new weight settled at the nose of the boat, enough to rock it. Through half-shut eyes, Patrick saw huge wings fold in on themselves, and terrible claws dig into the soggy wood of the bow-seat. A shaggy gray head with a bat's scooping ears twisted slowly toward him.

"What are you doing down here?" this strange harpy asked him.

In the dream, it was easier to speak, even with his parched and burning throat.

"Where else would I go?"

"Farther on, and farther up." The gray-haired harpy spread tattered wings and flapped once—the mighty gust blew Patrick's wet hair back. "Come on," she said. "Fly."

"I can't," Patrick answered, as though this wasn't a plain fact but something that needed to be explained. "I haven't got wings, have I?"

The harpy craned her neck, looking him over curiously.

"No—no, you haven't." She clicked reproachfully. "Tsk, tsk. What a pity."

A thought struck Patrick, and he tried weakly to sit up from the boat's bottom.

"But you could carry me," he started to say. "On your back, or with your—"

An indignant ruffle of gray fur interrupted. "You know I cannot. You've come so far on your own already. Now you want to be carried by this final measure?"

Patrick scowled. "What do you care, anyhow? You're not even here. I'm only dreaming."

The old harpy looked him up and down, as if measuring him with her eyes. "No, you're not dreaming," she said. "You're dying. Fly away. You'll die if you stay here."

"You're mocking me," Patrick answered. "You know I can't."

Her wings lifted then fell in two humps, the approximation of shrugging shoulders.

"Then I'll come back when you're dead," she offered. "I'll drink your blood and nibble the skin off your bleached bones. You won't mind, will you? You won't be needing it."

"Suit yourself," Patrick mumbled. He could feel himself drifting out of the dream, and he turned over on his side, facing away from this strange new passenger in his floating coffin. He curled inward like a shrimp, the gnawing ache in his belly sharpening and sharpening.

"Tell me something," he whispered. "If you're real,

or even if you aren't. Have you seen Stella? Or my mother, Fay. Are they safe? Are they together?"

The harpy kept her own silent council. Patrick tried again.

"Just tell me they really escaped," he begged. "Just tell me they're all right."

Still, no answer came. Patrick's eyes fell slowly shut.

"Do they..." he whispered. "Do they still think about me?"

The old harpy said nothing even to this. But this time, he felt her weight shift as she flapped and hopped toward the back of the boat, closer and closer to where he lay. A taloned foot came down hard between his shoulder blades; he could feel its steely grip testing his shirt, flexing open and closed experimentally, scraping through to his skin.

"And what of you?" her rasping voice asked. "Did you escape as well?"

Then her curving claws tore through his clothes and his flesh.

"Stupid boy," she muttered again and again. "*Fly. Fly.*"

CHAPTER 18
A GOOD MAN

IT WAS AGONY FOR AN INSTANT—BUT *only* for an instant.

Then his eyes cracked open, and the world was all-different. Night's curtain had come down, but the colors were wrong, sharper in some places, hazier in others. The dark seemed to shimmer—at first, Patrick thought this was the twinkling of the stars, but it was the very air around him that glittered now, the very fabric of the night itself. The sea lay flat and still around his little boat, though a constant soothing wind breathed across his skin. It nuzzled against him, nudging encouragingly, bearing him up like a comforting hand.

Without meaning to, he sat up—his thirst had vanished, as well as the ever-present ache and itch of his reddened, too-tight skin. His clothes lay in ribbons all around him, scattered at the bottom of the boat. But there was no blood. The wolf-skin lay draped across his shoulders, but somehow he could feel the wind's touch through it, like somebody breathing against his cheek, raising all the little hairs on the backs of his arms and neck.

The wind, the wind—

It *was* lifting him after all, drawing him upward until he stood teetering in the boat with his legs splayed, his bare toes gripping the rocking gunwales. He laughed in sheer disbelief; his whole body felt buoyant, over-light —like he'd been yoked to the ground his entire life and had just now laid down a crushing load. All weakness had left him. The only pain remaining in his whole body blazed between his shoulders, where the old harpy had slashed him open with her claws. But even this felt new and strange and electric. The pain sharpened him, pulling the very stars above him closer, or him nearer to them.

Again, the wind prodded into his back, with such force this time that his feet nearly left the gunwales altogether. It was impossible. And yet—Patrick tilted his face toward the moon and spread his arms out wide, letting the night sea-breeze catch inside the wolf-skin like a billowing sail...

The wolf-skin was no skin at all. And his arms were not arms.

They were wings.

Long and chiropteran and flexing, they stretched away from each shoulder, the color of dusk, the color of summer storms. They moved against the wind as though by some instinct of their own, holding him steady but also lifting him teasingly skyward. And though they seemed to obey his commands, he understood somehow that these new wings did not belong to him alone. There was a second command beneath his own, another guiding will, thrilling alongside him at this new sensation. Across every inch of their sleek fur, he could revel in the *intent* of the moving wind—its very desire, its warm and breathing *need*.

It wanted him. *It wanted him to fly.*

Experimentally, Patrick pushed up from the boat with his feet. Instantly, the sea dropped away beneath him, spiraling down in a dark rush as the wind filled his outstretched wings and pulled him whooping and wheeling up into the night. The horizon dipped and danced, spinning crazily as he cartwheeled through clouds and starlight, and when he screamed out in joy and terror in equal measure, his voice rioted from his lips in a high, wild screech.

To his surprise, another screeching voice called back. A long shadow darted across the moon, tucked its gray wings—and dove straight for him.

The gale of her passage buffeted Patrick like an ocean wave, sending him sprawling through the air. The old gray-haired harpy only laughed, rising again to meet him, leveling off and beating the air with her own wings so they coasted together above the glassy expanse of the sea. On the boat, her back had hunched with age, but airborne, her wings stretched out luxuriously, her white shoulders rippling with powerful muscle. Her long, thin hair streamed behind her like a kite's tail, pulled back from her face—but it was only when her eyes crinkled at him with that old mischievous twinkle that he saw who she truly was.

"Grandmother," he gasped.

Her reply came not in words but in a screech of gigantic delight. She flapped her wings once, swirling around her grandson in a tight circle until she had wrapped herself around his whole body. She pressed wrinkling lips to his cheek, then released them before they plummeted too low and plunged into the sea.

"I found my wings!" she crowed. "And look at you— now you've found yours!"

"I'm dreaming again, aren't I?" he yelled above the wind.

But his grandmother only smiled, showing fangs longer and yellower than Stella's or even his mother's.

"That pain between your shoulders," she said. "Does that feel like a dream?"

"So it was you. They come from you."

Her grin widened. "A gift—one you needed very badly, I think. Do you like them?"

Patrick's heart leapt inside his ribs—but behind that lurked a terrible ache, the cold sudden relief of a wound closing inside him. Tears began to flow, boiled away by the hot wind.

"I thought..." he said. "I thought I'd lost you."

"Never for even a moment," soothed his grandmother. "Ten years now, I've been watching over you, from high up among the clouds. I think maybe you even saw me once, above that pasture. But I didn't dare come any closer, even though I wanted to every day. Not even to let you know I was all right. I hope you understand why."

"That was you as well." He dried his eyes on a cloud-colored wingtip. "Now I know this can't be real. I'm dreaming. I died on that boat."

"Not quite," she sang out. "Almost, but not quite. You managed to find yourself just in time. Now—come on, come on, come on, we've got to keep moving!"

With only the slightest adjustment of her enormous wings, she rocketed ahead of him, soaring up higher and higher, pale as the moon against the welcoming dark.

Patrick flapped his wings as well, struggling to keep pace with her speed. "Where are we going?" he called after her, which his grandmother answered with an echoing shriek.

"Higher, always higher!" she said. "Farther on, and farther up!"

He caught her more quickly than he expected—her passage seemed to leave a kind of track in the air, leading him forward and also pulling him after her. Flying at her back, he could move faster than he'd believed it was possible for any living thing to travel. Spit dried on his teeth; his eyes narrowed to slits against the wind. And they were still climbing, lifting away from the flashing sea into the clouds that crowded the endless staring stars.

As they passed through these, by degrees Patrick became aware of another shape flying beside them, slipping in and out of the clouds like a prowling wolf among the trees. With a laugh, he tilted his body, veering away from his grandmother's trail, chasing this intruder into the haze. They circled each other a while, taking turns playing the pursuer and the prey—until he blinked and lost track of his quarry, and found himself suddenly tackled into another winged embrace.

"So this is what kind of man you are," a voice crooned in his ear.

"Mother." His heart swelled, set singing by her voice. "Or—shall I call you Fay now?"

She led him free of the clouds so they could rejoin his grandmother. Now he could see her fully, under the milk-colored moonlight—silver-winged and slender-shouldered, sleek and powerful, with grasping claws tipping each dangling foot. Only in the face was she the mother he remembered, with the same dark hair and sad, shrewd eyes.

"Not Fay. Never Fay to you." She shook her head, her long ears swept back in a broad letter V. "Being your mother," she told him gently, "that was my only joy in Blackfrye. I'll never ask you to call me anything else."

He turned away from her splendor, his hair snapping against his cheeks.

"Mother, I've been a fool," he said. "I should have known. I should have been able to..."

She silenced him with a kiss on the side of his face. "I'm the one who should be sorry," she insisted. "I didn't mean to leave you. I was never going to leave that place without you, not unless you could get out on your own. But the men were coming, and Stella was still so hurt. We only had one chance..."

Her wings enveloped him quickly; once more, he was a child in the crush of her embrace, safe and precious and loved. "We always knew it would be you," she whispered to him. "We always knew you'd be the one to set us free."

"We...?" he asked, when she'd released him again.

She showed him every yellow fang—some yet stained with Old Matthew's blood.

"Did you think we're the only harpies in the sky?" she teased. "Now they all want to meet you, Patrick. Now they *all* know what you've done."

"Come on," urged his grandmother. "We've got to keep moving! Farther on..."

"...and farther up!" rejoined his mother.

Now they broke above the clouds. Here, the night shimmered more fiercely than ever, and the stars seemed to drift and scatter among them, instead of merely painting the bowl of the heavens. The other two harpies tilted their noses toward the moon and issued a series of saluting shrieks—and the reply clamored from all around them. It was like when Patrick had stood on the mountain-peak; harpies in their astonishing multitudes burst out from the darkness as if they had roosted among the stars themselves, each one joining the maelstrom of churning wings and claws and dark flashing eyes that started to fill the air around them. But now they were more daring, flashing past him so near that he could see their curious eyes examining him, their red mouths stretched in tight, jealous smiles. Their voices rose and fell in a shrill chorus, but now Patrick could understand them all.

"He's here," they crowed to each other, again and again. "It's him. It's him."

With another buffeting of their tremendous leather wings, his escorts soared higher, again leaving him to chase their tails. But instead, he slowed his pace, searching among all those pale, swirling faces, listening for one voice among the chorus. Anxious anticipation began to swell in his breast. He hoped; he hardly dared to hope. But then—

—but then ecstatic laughter broke through the tumult, and she appeared in the moonlight above him, tucking her wings and plunging at him like an osprey over water.

There was no time even to cry out. She tackled him full strength, nearly striking him down to the sea far below. He only just managed to catch himself, pulling out of a screaming tailspin before she met him again midair, swooping around and cuddling her warm body against his. He felt her frame twitch and shrink as she reduced into his embrace, her wings melting away so she could clasp her slender arms around his neck. Now they were careening through empty air together, but it hardly seemed to matter. She was *here*, really here, tucked tight to his chest, her lips inches from his neck.

In a faint and quivering voice, she said:

"*I didn't think I'd ever get to see you again.*"

There was only one way to answer this.

He joined his mouth with hers, pulling her into a kiss that had lived only in his dreams before that instant. She smiled against him and returned the kiss, tightening her grip as though she could draw herself entirely inside his skin. Then they broke apart and twirled on the wing, chasing each other across the sparkling night and between the storming wings of her sisters, before catching each other again and again, each joining ending with another splendid kiss. All around them, Stella's sisters screamed and cheered, and every so often, he caught a flash of his mother's knowing smile, watching from far on high—from farther on, and farther up.

But Stella was everything else.

The stars, the moon, the air beneath his wings—it was all her.

Now they were diving again, intertwined, their claws clutching, cocooning each other so nobody could tell where one's wings ended and the other's began. Their hair snarled around their faces; the howling wind snatched their breath away. Stella's face streamed, and when her lips moved, no sound escaped. So he pulled her close, speaking in her ear so his words belonged to her and her alone.

"I never thought you'd hear it," he said. "But—I love you, Stella."

"I never thought I'd get to say it," she replied, "but I love you, too."

Then, feeling overwhelmed her, and she could speak no more. So she kissed him, showed him her teeth, and kissed him again. Only when she pressed herself close against him did she find her voice once more. And once he'd heard those final few words, Patrick didn't care if they were flying or falling. He didn't care if they fell forever.

"Up here..." she whispered. "Up here, *we pluck our husbands from the earth.*"

Jacob Steven Mohr does not believe in human consciousness; his works emerge as though from the ether, fully formed and fully ominous. Selections of these can be observed in Cosmic Horror Monthly, Shortwave Magazine, Chthonic Matter Quarterly, Weird Horror Magazine, and The Best Horror of the Year Vol. 15. He exists in Columbus, Ohio.

Thank you for reading *Brides in the Dark*. We deeply appreciate our readers, and are grateful for everyone who takes the time to leave us a review. If you're interested, please visit our website to find review links. Your reviews help small presses and indie authors thrive, and we appreciate your support.

Other Horror Titles from Quill & Crow

Bury Me Cold & More Last Words, Jacob Steven Mohr

Where Dark Things Rise, Andrew K. Clark

Change & Other Terrors, Jim Horlock